The Sword, the

Garden, and the

Annals of the For

A fairy tale for children of all ages

By

Michael Phillips

THE AUTHOR

Best-selling novelist Michael Phillips is the author of many beloved books and series. Some of his most well-known are Shenandoah Sisters, Carolina Cousins, The Secret of the Rose, and The Journals of Corrie Belle Hollister. He has also dedicated his life to preserving and furthering the legacies of his two literary mentors, George MacDonald and C.S. Lewis. George MacDonald (1824-1905) is the Victorian Scottish author whose writings led C.S. Lewis to Christianity and whom Lewis called his spiritual "master." MacDonald's fantasies and fairy tales also provided the inspiration for Lewis's *The Chronicles of Narnia*. Phillips is the man who brought the works of George MacDonald back into print in the 1980s. His edited, republished and young reader editions, as well as his biography of MacDonald, introduced a new generation of readers to the forgotten Scotsman. Through the years Phillips' own writings have earned him a place in a literary lineage that extends from MacDonald to C.S. Lewis and into the present generation. Many have compared Phillips' afterlife fantasy *Hell and Beyond* to Lewis's *The Great Divorce* and MacDonald's *Lilith*. With *The Sword, the Garden, and the King*, Michael Phillips takes his stand beside his predecessors with a memorable "fairy tale for children of all ages." It is sure to be read and savored by many who love the Narnian tales and MacDonald's Curdie books and other fairy stories.

Grateful acknowledgment is given to my dear brother Nigel Halliday, whose creative brainstorming was an integral part of the early days of this book. He is a man who understands the eternal importance of knowing one's *true* name. Nigel's ideas and contributions have been invaluable and are sprinkled like gems throughout this tale. Surely there is no greater stimulus to the storyteller's art than a friend who shares the vision. I thank you, my friend!

The Sword, the Garden, and the King
Copyright © 2013 by Michael Phillips

.
Published 2013 by Yellowood House, an imprint of Sunrise Books

ISBN: 978-0940652705

DEDICATION

To the real life "Matthew,"
My grandson Matthew Phillips.

You have grown up since I wrote this for you and your
brother and sister. You are now nearly a man! May you
carry the legacy of your name with honor and courage,
and most importantly, may the Cloak of Humility protect
you all the days of your life.

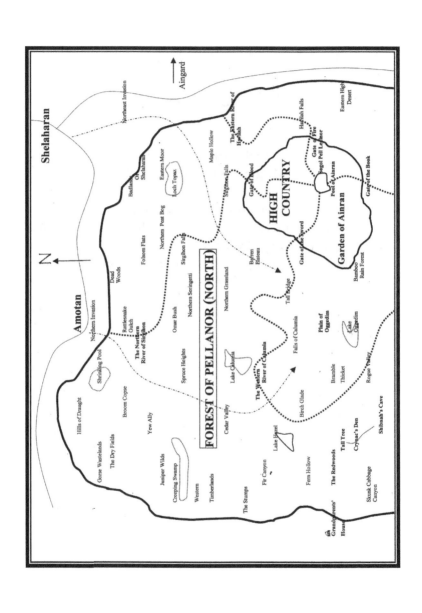

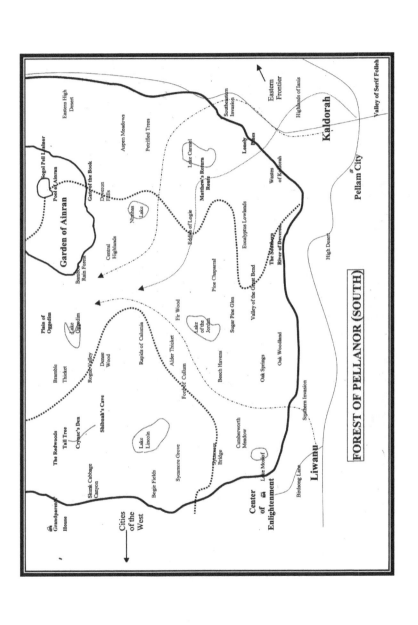

FOREST OF PELLANOR (SOUTH)

CONTENTS

ONE

Matthew Sees Into the Past...

or Maybe the Future

You can never tell how an adventure will begin. There are many different kinds of adventures, and this one begins with a boy called Matthew and a dream.

Actually it doesn't *begin* with his dream.

The dream got into his brain because of a conversation he remembered with his great-grandfather from a year before. His great-grandfather had been telling him about the world war in Europe from the last century. Their talk got all mixed up inside Matthew's mind with a story he was reading. Probably many of you have read that same book. Then there was also his great-grandfather's medal from the war, and—

Perhaps I should just tell you about the conversation, the book, the medal, and the dream. Then you can decide for yourself how Matthew's adventure began, and whether the dream was of the past...or the future.

"Opa, will you tell me a story?" said Matthew, jumping onto the couch beside a gray-haired man with a long white moustache and beard.

"I suppose I might, Matthew, my boy," replied the man. "What kind of story would you like?"

"A true story."

"Wouldn't you like a make-believe story?"

"I would rather hear about when you were a soldier."

The man chuckled. "Do you never tire of my stories of the war!"

"You were in it, Opa. How could I get tired of it? Tell me again about leaning out of airplanes. Why did you lean out?"

"I had to lean out because I was taking pictures of the ground below."

"Why didn't you just take them through the window?"

"I had to aim my camera straight down. The only way to do that was to lean out the open cockpit and look at the ground while I pointed my camera at what I wanted to photograph."

"Did you open the door?"

"A photographer's plane had no door on the passenger side."

Matthew's brother Timothy, who was nine years old, had been listening from across the room. He now came and jumped onto the couch with his brother.

"Do you think your sister would like to listen, too?" asked their great-grandfather.

"Susanna!" cried Timothy. "Opa's telling a story."

A six year old girl with blond hair scampered out of her bedroom toward them and climbed into her great-grandfather's lap.

"All right, then," said the man. "Where was I?"

"You were telling us about leaning out of the airplane," said Timothy. "Were you wearing a parachute?"

"No," laughed his great-grandfather. "But I was strapped in."

"You might have fallen, Opa," said Susanna.

"That's why I was strapped in!"

"Why were you taking pictures, Opa?" asked Matthew.

"Because we needed to see what the enemy was doing. Our cameras were like eyes surveying the landscape below. The cameras were so powerful they could see things that were invisible to ordinary sight."

"Like an eagle," said Timothy. "We learned about eagles in school. They have the strongest eyes of any animal in the world."

"That's just it, my boy. We were the eagles' eyes of the war, watchmen flying over the land. It was our job to protect our army."

"Owls and falcons have strong eyes, too," said Matthew.

"Yes they do...and hawks," replied the great-grandfather. "Most birds have keen eyesight. Perhaps they might be called watchmen, too, over the fields and meadows and woodlands where they live."

"They're just looking for food, aren't they, Opa?" said Timothy. "Like mice and rabbits and prairie dogs."

"Perhaps, Timothy, my boy. But did you ever stop to think that maybe they are also looking out for danger, to protect their lands from invasion in the same way that we were trying to protect Europe?"

"What could a bird do?"

"Sound the alarm, warn the other animals and the king of the land."

"Do animals really do that, Opa?" asked Susanna.

"Haven't you ever walked outside and heard crows start squawking and making a fuss? They're warning the other animals that humans are about."

"But we aren't their enemies," objected Matthew. "I would help the animals if they were in danger."

"Would you really help them if they were in trouble, Matthew, my boy?" asked his great-grandfather. His voice sounded more serious than if he were just telling a story.

"If I knew what to do."

3

"*Tell us more about the airplanes, Opa,*" said Timothy.

"*Did I ever show you the photographs I took when we flew over an erupting volcano?*"

"*No! Was it scary!*"

"*A little,*" laughed his great-grandfather. "*But we were high above it. The pilot of the airplane kept out of the way.*"

"*Did guns from the ground shoot at your plane?*"

"*A few times,*" nodded the old man. "*Now that was scary!*"

That's how Matthew's adventure started.

It was a year later now. He and Timothy and Susanna were leaving to visit their grandmother and grandfather again the following morning. They had not seen them since the previous summer. Their great-grandfather Robinson, whom they called *Opa*, lived with their grandparents and was always full of stories and eager to play games when they came to visit.

All three could hardly sleep for excitement about going again to the house in the country next to the big wood. Matthew had been thinking about it all day. He was still thinking about it when he went to bed. That's why his great-grandfather's story from the year before about leaning out of airplanes had come back to him.

As he lay in bed thinking about tomorrow's trip, Matthew was reminded of the peculiar things both his grandfather and great-grandfather often said, that there were wars going on around them all the time, though not the same kind of war. They were not in danger from guns and bombs, he said. It was an invisible war that most people were unaware of.

Matthew hadn't understood much about all that. He was only thirteen when listening to his great-grandfather's airplane story. Now he was a whole year older.

He rolled over in his bed and yawned a time or two. He found his place again in the book he had been reading.

Silly little bleater! he read. *Go home to your mother and drink milk. What do you understand of such things? But you others, listen. Tash is only another name for Aslan. All that old idea of us being right and the Calormenes wrong is silly. We know better now. The Calormenes use different words but we all mean the same thing. Tash and Aslan are only two different names...*

But Matthew could not keep his eyes open.

He closed the book and rolled over and set it on his nightstand. There lay the medal his great-grandfather had given him last year. He had placed it there so he would not forget to pack it in the morning.

Finally Matthew turned off his light. Within minutes he was fast asleep.

A few hours later his dream began.

It was impossible to tell whether the chaotic din echoed as a memory from a time far in the past, or from a more recent battle.

There could be no doubt a war was on. But what kind of war?

The clash of steel upon steel was certainly made by swords. Vague figures on horseback wearing coats of mail and helmets of armor galloped blurrily across the landscape. Arrows whizzed by in every direction. But the gunfire and explosions of mines and bombs, and the occasional shrill drone of a diving fighter plane also made it clear that not just ancient combat was involved. So too was the advanced technology of modern warfare.

It seemed a war for all ages. But how could swords and arrows survive against guns, airplanes, and tanks?

The combatants' cries, too, were strange. A terrible racket mingled the pandemonium of animal shrieks and brays and squawks and roars with human shouts in queer disorderly clamor. There were children scurrying about, and old men calmly watching, awaiting the season when bravery would be required of them again. Courageous women and mothers took their places with swords in hand and fire in their eyes against those usurping the family order.

What a strange battle it was—animals and people, children and women and old men, swords and helmets of steel along with guns and bombs!

An airplane roared down, spraying machine gun fire like rain. Scattering from its barrage were soldiers in uniform, but also a wild assortment of foxes, rats, sheep, beavers, pigs, elk, cows, cats, goats, dogs, chickens, mountain lions, camels, giraffes, and birds flying in a tumult overhead.

The plane came low. Bombs screamed toward the ground. Huge craters exploded out of the earth. The ground trembled as the plane soared high and quickly flew out of sight.

More explosions. A herd of elephants rumbled by, shaking the ground with thick-padded feet of walking thunder. Behind them rose a chant: HO, RUMBLE, RUMBLE, RUMBLE.

But they did not long remain elephants. Gradually from amid their hulking bodies emerged a fleet of steel-armored tanks rumbling across the uneven terrain. Where long pachydermal trunks had coiled and uncoiled with slow probing fluidity now great cannons swiveled on clattering metal machinery and exploded fire.

Everywhere on the battlefield, men and animals, infantrymen and dogs and panthers and skunks and cats dove into foxholes to escape the artillery fire. Birds scattered in a frenzy for the treetops.

The images of battle grew weird, grotesque, other-worldly.

Another plane screamed into view and dove steeply down. As it approached, gradually it changed. Its wings spread and widened and took on life of their own. Feathers replaced steel and began to flutter. Where the glass of the cockpit had been, two huge eyes peered out, panning back and forth surveying the landscape. They were not a camera's eyes but keen living seeing eyes.

Where an airplane had approached now soared a massive peregrine falcon, huge and fearsome. It swooped low over the battle as if coming in for a landing.

As the falcon-plane neared the ground, shrieks and ear-piercing cries filled the air. Great wolves jumped high, mouths wide and fangs bared to grab hold of its feet. Huge cats of some kind leaped higher than the wolves with claws outstretched to snatch the falcon from the air. Crows, flickers, buzzards, treacherous owls, geese with death in their eyes, and hawks came screeching and cawing to attack the falcon from every side.

Everywhere sounded the phantasmagoric jumble of gunfire, explosions, clanking swords, human shouts, and the neighing of horses and braying of donkeys. Occasionally the roar of a lion or tiger could be heard, then the squealing of pigs. A hundred more grunts and yowls and bleats gave off a frenzied caterwaul of pandemonium.

A terrible howl momentarily drowned out the rest. One of the wolves, blood pouring from its back, was grabbed and lifted high by the peregrine's razor-sharp talons. The falcon threw the wolf mercilessly to its death on the jagged rocks below.

The falcon's head swerved in a half circle, then cried out in a squawky bird voice of command, "Get up,"it said, "get high!"

He swooped low in a great arc to rally the few who were left with him. The falcon's allies were a ragtag collections of mice and prairie dogs and a few dogs and raccoons and sheep and beaver and deer. "The trees are our protection," he cried. "The great tree...get to the tall tree. Get up...you must get further up!"

His exhortation did not seem unreasonable at the time, even though everyone knows that dogs and deer and sheep cannot climb trees. But everything was happening too fast to think about that.

Surging against the falcon's band came a much larger army—fierce, strong, menacing...wolves, tigers, bears, rhinoceroses, bulls, lions, mammoths, hippopotamuses, and eagles. Behind them, overseeing the charge that must surely lay waste to all who stood in its path, stood a man whose mane of white gave him the appearance of an angel of light. He cried to his mighty force:

"Further in...move further in! Onward and inward. The inheritance of the forest is ours! In to the inheritance...further in...further in!"

Whatever weird kind of battle this was, it was certainly like nothing recounted in the history books of the boy in whose mind the images were reverberating with bizarre reality.

It was a battle against those trying to get further up and those trying to get further in.

Now you can see how this battle of Matthew's dream had come from the words of the book he had just read mingled with those of his great-grandfather's story about taking pictures from airplanes.

The FURTHER UPPERS under command of the peregrine falcon were trying to reach the safety of the tall tree. But the invading FURTHER INNERS led by the man of light was surging deeper into the forest to prevent them.

In his desperation to rally his assortment of creatures to safety, the falcon flew too low. Suddenly the archers from Kaldorah joined the snapping wolves and clawing cats.

Hundreds of deadly arrows filled the sky aimed at the great bird's underside. It was too late for the falcon to swoop out of their path.

Feathers flew and a great cry rent the forest. The falcon wobbled down like a crash-landing plane, skidding onto its belly then tipping to its side. One wing was broken, an arrow protruded from its shoulder.

Cries of victory erupted from the wolves and cats. Their army surged with knives and swords aloft, teeth dripping with thirst for blood, to finish what it had begun.

Suddenly an eerie quiet descended like a blanket of silence over the battle. Every creature paused and looked toward the mountain in the distance. Their eyes beheld a giant of a man, fully clad in the armor of an ancient warrior. His face was obscured by a closed helmet of gold.

A great cheer rose from the forest people.

From somewhere a choir sang the familiar refrain: THE LIGHT IS DAWNING, THE LIE IS BROKEN!

But the prophetic song from that other land, accompanied by shouts of joy on the field of battle, lasted but a moment.

The forest and field and archers and tanks and airplanes faded. All became ghostly quiet, now inside an enclosed den or cave of some kind. Overhead a roof of compacted leaves and branches let in neither light nor rain. It might have been a nest high in the tree where the falcon had been urging his forces. Yet underfoot lay hard packed dirt. It had once been some animal's home.

It was empty now. The fire in the grate was cold. The place smelled musty and abandoned. Weeds and bramble vines poked through roof and walls. A table in the center of the room was overturned, several chairs broken. Glasses and plates and other furniture were scattered about in bits. Everywhere were signs of destruction. Whoever had ravaged the place, they had done their job thoroughly.

A few feathers were strewn over the dirt floor. Traces of blood were splattered near them. Something sinister had happened here. But no trace of animal or human body remained.

A sound came from outside. Someone, or something approached. Whatever evil had visited this place, the danger might still be lurking close by. It grew louder, then all at once—

Suddenly Matthew Robinson awoke, breathing hard.

He was sitting up in bed, sweating, surrounded by darkness.

He reached over and turned on the light of his nightstand. He glanced at the clock. It was two-thirty-five.

His eyes fell on the book he had been reading before falling asleep—the seventh in the well-known Englishman's series that gave inklings of another world and of the adventures of those lucky eight children and two grown-ups who had been fortunate enough to visit it.

Matthew's mind slowly came back into focus out of his dream. Beside the book, his eyes came to rest again on the medal beside the book. It was one of his most treasured possessions, a World War II medal of valor given him by his great-grandfather the year before. He had gotten it out yesterday so that he would remember to put it in his suitcase.

By now Matthew realized what you and I already know, that the events of the book, and the reminder of his great-grandfather's stories about the war got into his brain, too, and led to his dream about animals and war and peregrine falcons and airplanes.

He took in several deep breaths, lay his head back on his pillow, and tried to go back to sleep.

And though you may think that it was only a dream, it was actually far more than that. Usually dreams are mere fanciful nonsense. But sometimes they are sent as omens of things to come.

Matthew didn't know it yet, but that was exactly what kind of dream he had just had. It was a dream intended to tell him—not *exactly*, of course, but in a dream sort of way—what was going to happen when he went to his grandparents' house the next day.

The adventure of his life was right around the corner!

TWO

The Two Prairie Dogs

Matthew, Timothy, and Susanna arrived at their grandparents' house in the country the following afternoon. You might think they would be tired after a long airplane trip and ride from the airport. But they were anxious to roam about the big house they hadn't seen for a year. Matthew and Timothy didn't even bother to open their suitcases before dashing outside with their football and soccer ball. There was a big field next to the house with a tall single oak tree in the middle of it. There they could run and play and kick to their heart's content.

A plate of fresh chocolate chip cookies and glasses of cold milk brought them inside soon enough. Susanna was already seated at the kitchen table, a cookie in her hand and a white milk mustache on her lip, chattering away to her grandmother.

"Here you are, boys," said their grandmother as they ran inside and scooted two chairs to the table.

"Where are Grandpa and Opa?" asked Timothy as he bit into one of the big chewy cookies.

"Down in Grandpa's workshop, I believe," answered Mrs. Robinson. "They were in the library a moment ago, but I heard them going downstairs. They were talking about some special book binding project. You know how your grandfather is about his books!"

Everyone knows how a little exercise followed by a snack, especially after a long trip, can make you sleepy. It wasn't long before ten year old Timothy and seven year old Susanna were being led by their grandmother to their rooms. They were soon fast asleep.

But Matthew was fourteen. This was no time for naps! Naps were for children not fourteen year olds. No sooner had he swallowed the last of the milk in his glass than he was running back outside.

Mr. and Mrs. Robinson, along with Opa Robinson, lived on the edge of a great forest. When he was there the year before, Matthew had only played on the fringes of it. Now he was older and braver. So while his brother and sister slept, Matthew went out exploring.

Beyond the solitary oak and across the field rose the towering redwoods and fir and spruce of the great forest. They were taller than any trees near where he lived.

A momentary chill swept through him as he neared the edge of the field and looked up toward the tallest of them. Matthew did not stop to think what it meant. If he had, he might have recognized it as the sign that something important was about to happen.

Matthew wandered in among the thick shadows of the trees. His exploration on this day, even though it was but for a short time, was unlike earlier visits. The forest seemed speaking unknown secrets he had never noticed before. The trees and sounds were different. The fragrances were full of mysterious perfume.

Matthew soon found himself deeper into the wood than he had ever gone. He sensed the forest calling to his heart, though he didn't know what it was trying to say. The few birds and animals he saw seemed almost to be looking at him. A sparrow flew down close, sat on a branch and stared at him a moment before flying away. A little while later a blue jay did the same. Then a squirrel. The animals almost seemed to be watching him. His eyes saw with greater clarity, too, clearer than he imagined it possible to see. When he looked high into the trees, he could make out every leaf and branch.

But his new forest eyesight wasn't quite as keen as he thought. Matthew wasn't seeing *everything*. For high in the trees, an occasional fluffy movement of reddish-brown and gray entirely escaped his notice.

Of course the animals who were following him up in the treetops were very skilled at staying out of sight. Their Forest had recently become a dangerous place. Because of that they had learned to scurry over the ground and flit from tree to tree without being seen.

Though Matthew had no idea of it, he was being watched. The two prairie dogs high above him—Ginger and Spunky—were no ordinary prairie dogs. They were the watchmen of the Forest, and had been sent on a vital assignment to help save the Forest from a serious threat. They had been commissioned by He Who Rules, the King of the Forest, to watch for a human boy who would come to help rescue the Forest children who had been lured away from their families. These missing children were part of a plot to seize control of the Forest. The danger right now was particularly great because He Who Rules was away on an important mission, though nobody knew what it was.

This was not the first time they had seen Matthew. Ginger had been sent out of the Forest a year before and had first seen him then. He was finally convinced that Matthew was indeed the one they were looking for. Now they had to make contact with him and convince him to help.

After walking awhile, Matthew realized he had been gone a long time. He should probably go back. He turned around and retraced his steps. As soon as he left the canopy of the trees and walked back into the sunlight, his senses returned to normal.

He cast one last gaze back toward the wood, then hesitated a moment. For the short time he was in the forest, he felt like he had been in a whole different world.

He was thoughtful and quiet the rest of the day. He could not forget the strange feelings that had come over him among the tall trees.

As soon as Matthew disappeared into the house, the two prairie dogs, who had followed him all the way back to the edge of the wood, fell into a spirited discussion.

"I think he is the one," declared Ginger in a high squeaky voice.

"How can you be sure it's him?" said Spunky. "It's been a year since he was here."

"I don't know," replied Ginger. "But he was moving in the right direction, toward the tree. The King said that would be one of the signs—that we should wait until he came to the Tall Tree."

"But he didn't go that far."

"Maybe he will next time. I am certain he's the boy we've been waiting for. Look how he has grown since last year. And he loves the wood more than ever."

That evening, as they sat around the fireplace in the house, Matthew told the others about his walk in the woods.

"The forest felt different, Grandpa," he added.

"How so?" asked Grandpa Robinson.

"Bigger, quieter, louder," answered Matthew, "brighter, the smells deeper, the sounds full of life. When I heard the breeze rustling through the leaves, I almost thought the trees were trying to say something."

"Trees can't talk, Matthew!" laughed Timothy. He was the practical one of the family.

"What did they say, Matthew?" asked Susanna, gazing with wide eyes at her older brother. The very fact that he had dared venture into the forest seemed to her more amazing than she could imagine. Susanna thought her brothers were the bravest boys in the whole world. To her, Matthew had already had a great adventure. But in fact, his adventures were only beginning!

"I said *almost*," replied Matthew to his sister's question. "I couldn't really hear them saying anything. It just felt like they wanted to. My eyes seemed different, too, like there were things I might have been able to see, if I just *could* have seen them. But I couldn't quite."

A peculiar expression came over both the elder Robinson men's faces. It contained the hint of a knowing smile between father and son. Matthew's great-grandfather then proceeded to tell them a story about the war when he was a young man.

"Sometimes maybe the land does have secrets to tell," Opa Robinson began. "When I was in the war, I often felt that the animals, perhaps even the trees and fields, sensed that a fight was on for the survival of their land."

"How could you tell, Opa?" asked Susanna.

"I don't know, Susanna," he replied. "There was a sadness in the air. When it rained, it seemed that great tears were being shed because of the fighting, and because the land was not at peace."

"Tell us about the volcano, Opa," insisted Timothy.

"All right, lad," laughed his great-grandfather. "We had taken off that morning from Naples…"

THREE

What Happened at the Tall Tree

With visions of his great-grandfather's story and his walk into the wood swirling through his mind as he fell asleep, Matthew had another dream. But this was a happy dream of a land at peace.

Matthew dreamed about the Forest. Now it was truly *alive*. He could hear what the trees were saying. He could *see* what he only sensed before. He saw animals and their families and houses—all sorts of strange and interesting houses—from underground burrows to rabbit warrens in thick brambles, birds' nests and beaver lodges and foxes' dens…talking animals in tree houses, and all manner of creatures coming and going, gathering nuts and roots and berries and other things to eat and taking them to those who had none. The whole forest was a beehive of energy and activity, with happy sounds everywhere of families at work and play. Even the rabbits and foxes and sheep and mountain lions and deer and cougar were friends. Just as the dream began to fade, he saw Mrs. Rabbit paying a visit to Mrs. Fox with a container of hedgerow berries she had picked next to the warren where she lived. Then Mrs. Rabbit and Mrs. Fox parted with smiles like the best of friends. They didn't exactly hug each other, because of course rabbits and foxes use all four of their legs to walk, and had no extra arms to hug with. But you could tell that they would have given each other affectionate hugs if they had known how. Sometimes they sit on their haunches, but it would be awkward to try to hug like that.

When Matthew woke up the next morning the dream was so vivid in his brain that he could not wait to explore the Forest again. The moment breakfast was over, he jumped up from the table.

"May I go out into the Forest, Grandpa?" he asked excitedly.

"I suppose so, my boy," replied his grandfather. "What are you going to do?"

"I had a dream about it last night. I want to see if anything I dreamed is still there."

"Don't be silly, Matthew," said Timothy from across the table. "Dreams aren't real." Sometimes maybe Timothy was *too* practical.

"Don't be so sure, Timothy, lad," said Opa Robinson from the other side of the table. "You can never tell what might actually be real in the end." Again a knowing smile passed between grandfather and great-grandfather.

Matthew turned and ran for the door.

But practical though he was, Timothy wasn't about to miss out on anything that promised to be an adventure. He jumped down and hurried after Matthew. "I'm coming, too!" he shouted.

"And me!" chimed in Susanna, scooting off her chair.

"I think it might be best for the two of you to stay with Grandma and me," said Mr. Robinson.

"Why, Grandpa?" asked Timothy as Matthew disappeared outside. "I want to see the forest."

"I'm sure you will, my lad. But we are meant to have some adventures alone, and some we are meant to share."

Matthew was already running across the field to the edge of the wood. He slowed as he gazed up at the high treetops.

A chill swept through him, though it was a bright sunny morning, as if he was about to enter a world that held secrets he was about to discover. When he came to the first trees growing beside the field, he slowed to a walk. The shadows and the huge tree trunks and the branches and leaves overhead gradually swallowed him as he entered the Forest.

He turned and looked back. Less than ten feet away he could still see the sunlight and green grass of the open field he had just left. The red walls of his grandmother's and grandfather's house sat in the distance. Then he turned again into the wood. After a few more steps, he cast another glance behind him. The house and field had disappeared. All about him in every direction were trees. He knew the story of the coats turning into prickly snow-covered fir branches better than just about any story in the world. Yet somehow it never crossed his mind that something similar was happening to him. It had happened so gradually he had hardly noticed. This had always seemed a perfectly normal wood. So it did not occur to him that something very peculiar was happening. Nor did he stop to consider that every experience in a new world is unlike any other. When it comes to worlds different than our own, all the rules change.

You might think, finding himself alone and, as it seemed, suddenly far away from where he had been only a few moments before, that Matthew would have been afraid. But except for a brief tingle, not of fear exactly but of exhilaration, he did not think that there might be danger ahead. He was still too full of his happy dream of the night before to think of the Forest as anything but alive with delightful creatures and happiness and goodness everywhere.

But the Forest did not feel like his dream. He was surrounded by a deep quiet. There was not a breath of wind. Not a leaf rustled above him.

He walked on, slowly, feeling many of the same sensations he had on the previous day. Though it was now *much* quieter. There were no birds or squirrels about. The whole Forest seemed waiting for something. Gradually an eerie feeling came over Matthew that he was not alone.

He walked for perhaps ten minutes. At last he heard a sound — the faint rustling of a branch above him.

He glanced up toward it. All fell quiet again. As he continued on, Matthew felt dampness on his forehead. He realized that his whole face was wet. But why? He was not perspiring. He glanced about and saw that the air was full of a fine mist, so light and fine he had hardly noticed.

Had it started to rain, Matthew wondered. Yet wherever he looked through the trees, the sky overhead was blue.

After walking a long time, Matthew stopped again. Ahead of him he saw the most enormous tree imaginable, bigger and taller than any tree he had ever seen in his life. It looked like a great redwood, but was different, too — like a species made up of *every* kind of tree.

Matthew stood and gazed at the trunk, then walked around it and stood close and tried to stretch his arms around it. But his hands didn't even go halfway. He stood back and looked toward the sky. Staring straight up made him dizzy. He could not see the top of the huge tree. Its trunk disappeared amongst the branches and leaves surrounding it. Surely it must be the tallest tree in the Forest.

Again he heard a noise like before. This time it was closer down. Matthew spun around in time to see a reddish-brown bushiness disappear along a branch and scurry up the trunk.

He stood and stared after it. A few seconds later two eyes sparkled against the dark of the trunk. Then he saw an animal creeping down the trunk of the tree toward him. It was larger than any squirrel or chipmunk he had ever seen, as big as a large cat or even a small dog. Could it be a groundhog, he wondered. He had never seen one in the wild. But what would a groundhog be doing in a tree! As his eyes met the animal's eyes, another tingle surged through Matthew's body. He knew that the animal was looking at him with eyes of understanding and knowing.

He was in for an even greater shock. For suddenly the animal spoke.

"You are Matthew," it said. From the inflection of its voice, Matthew could not tell if it was a statement or a question. It hardly mattered. The shocking thing was that an animal had spoken to him!

He stared up at the two eyes in disbelief, then slowly nodded.

"Yes, I am Matthew Robinson," he said. "How do you know my name?"

"We have been watching you," replied the animal. "We have been waiting for you to come to this tree. We have been following you ever since you entered the Forest. We have been waiting for you to be ready.

"Ready for what?"

"For all that will be required of you."

"Required of me...what do you mean? Required by who?" Matthew should have said by *whom*, but right now he was too astonished to think about the grammar lessons he had learned in school.

In fact, Matthew didn't really believe this was happening at all! Animals didn't talk. Groundhogs couldn't climb trees! Nor were chipmunks as big as dogs! He must be back in his dream.

He had no more time to think about it because now the animal spoke again.

"By the King of the Forest, of course," he said.

"I don't live in the Forest," said Matthew, deciding to play along. He would have a little fun with this animal, whatever it was, even if he was still lying in his bed back at his grandfather's house! "Whoever you're talking about, he's not my King."

"Oh, isn't he!" rejoined the animal impatiently, wondering how a human could be so stupid. "You will find out soon enough that he is your King as well as mine. And he wants you to help us. That's why I've been watching you."

"I just went for a walk in the woods near my grandfather's house," said Matthew.

"I took you for smarter than that," said the animal. "Don't you know that everything is planned. You were *meant* to come here. You are the King's boy, and I suggest you start acting like it."

Matthew was a little shocked. He didn't altogether like being put in his place like that.

"I know what you are thinking," said the animal, "that you are dreaming again, and that none of this is real."

Matthew laughed. "How did you know?"

All at once there was a great scurrying and the animal scampered the rest of the way down the tree. Before Matthew knew what was happening, it leapt to the ground, ran around behind him, and bit him in the back of the leg.

"Ouch!" cried Matthew. "That hurt. Why did you do that!"

"To wake you up, if you think you are dreaming," said the animal, more than a little annoyed. "But you *aren't* dreaming," he added. "Maybe a little sting in your leg will show you how serious this is."

Suddenly from above Matthew's head came another flurry of motion. Before he knew it, he was spinning around gazing down at *another* animal just like the first that came up as high as his knees. He didn't know if they could stand on their hind legs, but if so they could probably stand up as tall as his waist!

Along with the reddish-brown animal who had just bit him, the second was of the lightest and fluffiest gray. But Matthew hardly had time to take them in, because now the newcomer spoke.

"What's wrong with you, boy," he said "Aren't you listening? Ginger told you that you had come to this tree because the King needs you. Now you listen or he will have to bite you again."

Finally Matthew realized this was no dream. These animals were *really* talking to him!

"I am sorry," he said. "I was just surprised. I've never met a talking animal before. I've never met a talking *anything* before...well, a talking whatever kind of animal you are. If you don't mind me asking, what *are* you, anyway."

"Prairie dogs, of course. What did you think we were?"

"I don't know. You're so big. And what are you doing climbing in trees like squirrels?"

"We learned how. Not all prairie dogs can, but it's not so hard once you get used to it. Squirrels are our cousins, anyway. Why shouldn't we be able to do anything they can?"

"Do all the animals in this Forest talk?"

"Of course," replied the prairie dog called Ginger. "But they speak many languages. Sometimes it is hard to understand the birds. But never mind about that. Can you climb?"

"You mean a tree—yes. If the branches are low enough to grab hold of."

"Do you mean you can't walk up the trunk?"

"I don't have claws on my hands like you do. I have to use branches for my hands and feet."

"Hmm, that is going to make it a little inconvenient.— Spunky, see if you can find a tree we can use. He obviously can't fit down in one of our burrows. And we can't stand around talking on the *ground* of all places. We might be *seen*."

The second prairie dog scampered away. It didn't take him long to return. He then led the way and soon Matthew was climbing up through the branches of another tree. It was much smaller than the big one. Its branches grew close enough to the ground that Matthew reached the lowest ones and got started up the trunk. The two prairie dogs were surprised at how slow he climbed. Every few seconds, after scurrying their way up, they stopped to wait for him. And Matthew was surprised how they could scurry about in the trees as if they were squirrels!

After five or six minutes, Matthew felt the tree beginning to sway from his weight.

"I think this is as high as I ought to go," he said. He was already so high that he was afraid to look down.

"What?" said the prairie dog called Spunky. "We're only halfway up."

"I think I am afraid to go higher."

"Afraid, what kind of a pr—"

"Spunky," interrupted Ginger sternly. "We were commanded not to use that word."

Ginger turned to Matthew.

"Well, then," he said, "this will have to do. I am certain you will become brave enough later for what you have to do."

"What *do* I have to do?" asked Matthew.

"Just save the Forest from the evil people who are trying to destroy it," replied Ginger. "I am still not certain why the King wants a boy. Why doesn't he just save us himself. But that is what the old legend says—*The wolf shall dwell with the lamb. And a little child shall lead them.*—So the King must know best."

"I'm *hardly* a little child."

"Neither are you anywhere close to a man."

"But I can't save the Forest," objected Matthew. "Even if I'm not a little kid, I'm still only here on a holiday. I'll just be here three weeks."

"We shall see about that. The King always knows what he is doing. I am certain that will be time enough. For now, make yourself comfortable on those branches. And listen carefully."

Four

The Crow, the Palace, and the King

Matthew went to sleep that night with his mind full of all that had happened in the Forest. He said nothing to Timothy or Susanna about what the prairie dogs had told him—though the looks his grandfather and great-grandfather both gave him made him wonder if they suspected something. But he didn't want to talk about it until he was quite *sure* he wasn't dreaming.

Matthew woke up the next morning to a strange sound. Someone was calling his name in a scratchy kind of voice.

"Matthew...Mathew Robinson. Wake up...wake up and come with me."

Now you might think by this time that Matthew would not have a hard time believing these strange happenings. He was a very smart boy, one of the smartest in his class at school. But he was very confused. You and I have to ask ourselves what *we* would think if animals started talking to us! We probably wouldn't believe it either.

Matthew looked around the room. The night had been very warm and he and Timothy had left the window open.

There stood a black crow on the open window sill regarding him "with an expression at once respectful and quizzical."

Timothy was awake by now, too.

"Did you hear that, Timothy!" asked Matthew excitedly.

"What—that old bird?" said Timothy, rubbing his eyes and looking toward the window.

"Yes! Did you hear what it said?"

"*Said?* I heard it squawking."

"Come, Matthew," the crow went on. "The king is waiting for you. Say nothing to anyone. Your mission is secret. None of your family must know."

A tendency to croak caused a certain roughness in his speech, but his voice was not disagreeable, and what he said, although conveying little enlightenment, did not sound rude.

"There…he did it again!" exclaimed Matthew. "Timothy, you must have heard him."

"I just heard a stupid old crow cawing at us."

Timothy jumped out of his bed and ran for the drawer where he had put his toys. He pulled out his plastic gun—the kind that shoots little arrows with rubber tips on the ends. He stuck in an arrow and shot it in the direction of the window.

"Timothy, stop!" cried Matthew.

"I don't like crows. It serves it right for trying to get into our room."

Matthew ran to the open window. The crow had flown off, but he saw it swooping down and landing on the lawn next to the house. It glanced back up at the window where Matthew was standing, then swiveled its head round over its shoulder and made a jerking motion in the direction of the field. It hopped a few steps, looked back again, and finally flew off toward the woods. Matthew knew the crow meant him to follow.

He had not even finished unpacking his suitcase yet. Quickly he grabbed a shirt and pair of trousers from it, dressed, dashed outside, and made for the field. When Matthew was halfway toward where he usually entered the woods, the crow swooped down near his head.

"This way," it said, "come this way. Follow me."

The crow led Matthew toward a different part of the Forest than where he had encountered the prairie dogs. Five minutes later, Matthew found himself again surrounded by trees. He stopped to catch his breath. The crow spiraled down amid the trees and landed in front of him. It had suddenly grown to about three times its size from the window sill. It stood as high as Matthew's knees!

"The king sent me to fetch you, boy," it said. "We have a long way to go—can you stay with me?"

"I don't know. I can't fly."

"I know that. What kind of nincompoop do you take me for? I'll lead the way, and you will run."

"I will try to keep up. But I haven't had breakfast yet," said Matthew, "and I am a little hungry. It will be hard to run a long distance on an empty stomach."

"I know you haven't had breakfast, boy. That's why the king sent me for you. He has a breakfast feast waiting for you."

So saying, the crow turned, took several hopping steps to get himself going, then flapped its wings and flew into the air. It went only a few hundred yards, then stopped and waited for Matthew to catch up. Again it flew ahead...and again...and again. Before long Matthew was panting so hard he didn't think he could possibly keep going much longer.

"Please, Mr. Crow," he said. "Could I stop and rest for a while. I am very tired."

"From that little run? You've hardly gone anywhere."

"You mean were not almost there yet?"

"Of course we're not almost there. We've only just begun. If you're getting weak I could find you a worm or baby mouse or something to tide you over."

"Ugh! No thank you," said Matthew. "I will wait for a proper breakfast."

Again they set out. The way seemed much farther than Matthew thought he could possibly run. The crow was leading him almost directly south, though Matthew wasn't thinking about the direction they were going. And they weren't as deep in the Forest as he thought. They were actually moving almost directly south only a half mile inside the western edge of the trees. After a long time they turned southwest and the Forest began to thin. The crow slowed and Matthew saw that they were approaching a clearing. As they got closer and the trees thinned more, he realized that it was not a clearing at all. They were leaving the Forest. A short way beyond the boundary of the trees sat a big brick house, surrounded by fields and gardens and vineyards and barns and paddocks. It looked like a farmhouse. All about were signs of bustle and activity.

The crow veered high up in the air and disappeared without another caw or croak. Matthew did not miss him because he had been a little cross during their journey. He was glad to be rid of him. But Matthew was not alone for long. A great menagerie of animals of all sorts and sizes and shapes now came running from the gardens and fields and barns and paddocks and house to welcome him. Matthew was surprised amongst the animals to see dozens of boys and girls near his own age, though with them were some older teen-agers and others even younger than his brother. Most had smiles on their faces, but strange to say a few looked sad.

There was a great clamor and commotion. Shouts of, "He has come, he has come at last! Welcome...welcome, Matthew Robinson!" were mixed up with barks and grunts and squeals and squawks and the chirping of more birds than you could count. Even the cows and horses and sheep in the fields beyond the house were *mooing* and *neighing* and *baaing* excitedly.

Matthew's first thought was that it seemed a very happy place. It reminded him of his happy dream about Mrs. Rabbit and Mrs. Fox being friends together. Maybe things in the Forest weren't so bad as the prairie dogs made it sound.

Following the throng of animals and children, a man now came out of the house and walked toward him. He was an ordinary human man by the looks of it, very tall with white hair and a white beard.

"Welcome, Prince Matthew!" he said with a smile of greeting on his face. He clasped Matthew's two shoulders, then bent down and kissed him on his two cheeks. "You have been expected. We rejoice to have you with us at last. I am Argon, king of the Forest."

Matthew was so overwhelmed that he was not really thinking clearly. So the first words that came out of his mouth were not what they might have been if he had thought about it for a moment.

"It looks like we are no longer in the Forest, sir," he said.

"A clever and perceptive young fellow you are!" smiled the man called Argon. "As why shouldn't a prince be. You are right, my palace sits at the edge of the Forest. But all the land you see, stretching north and east throughout the Forest and away south all the way to the sea, is my domain as well.— But enough of this," he added. "I know you are hungry from your journey. A breakfast feast in your honor awaits you in the palace!"

Matthew followed Argon toward the house, thinking to himself that it appeared very ordinary to be called a palace. It even seemed a little run down. But he *was* famished. If there was a feast inside he didn't care what the house looked like. And he had to admit he liked the sound of *Prince* Matthew.

He followed Argon inside. They were followed by the celebrating crowd of children and animals. Many of the younger children clustered close to him as they went. All around his feet scampered a multitude of small creatures.

The noise was so tumultuous that he could not make much of it. Many of the children and animals seemed to be chanting, *We are happy here…we are always happy here…everyone is happy here!* There was such a ruckus with Matthew at the center of it that he could not help laughing at being the focus of so much attention.

The house, or palace, seemed bigger on the inside that the outside. There were rooms everywhere, upstairs and downstairs. All the children that had been part of the crowd to greet him seemed to have their own rooms. Matthew wasn't quite sure about the animals. Some of them came inside and were walking about on their hind legs and talking with everyone as if they didn't even know they were animals. But the largest animals stayed outside.

A huge long table was laid out that looked like it could sit a hundred people. The smells coming from steaming platters all along it made Matthew almost delirious with hunger—eggs, sausages, bacon, warm breads, scones, silver platters piled with fruits and rolls and cakes, others with meats and jams and tarts and puddings.

He was led to the head of the table. He was obviously the guest of honor. Argon sat at the far end. All the animals and boys and girls scurried to their places. There were just exactly enough chairs for everyone.

Several of the teen-age boys and girls remained standing as the others scooted in their chairs with great bumping and sliding and adjusting. When everybody was settled, the three serving boys and three girls walked about the table pouring drinks into everyone's cups. In front of Matthew and Argon sat ornate silver goblets. Into these two of the older girls poured some kind of frothing, creamy liquid. It bubbled and foamed and steamed and gave off an aroma such as Matthew had never smelled in his life. It went straight to his head and made him think high thoughts about being a prince and ruling over great lands and dominions and having servants to do all he commanded. When the two goblets at the ends of the table were full, the servers proceeded to pour all the rest of the company glasses of some kind of red juice.

At length Argon rose. He lifted his goblet high across the table toward Matthew. All the animals and other children lifted their glasses of juice.

"Rise, Prince Matthew!" he said. "We welcome you, and we now toast your future among us."

Matthew rose and picked up the goblet in front of him.

"Drink, Prince Matthew, of the Elixir of Wisdom."

Argon lifted his drink to his lips. Matthew did the same and drank. All those about the table drank deeply from their glasses.

The fragrant liquid entered Matthew's mouth. As it glided slowly down his throat, a warm sensation of peace and power and well-being filled his body. What the drink was made of he could not guess—though it was thick and creamy, with reminders of vanilla and milky chocolate and brown sugar and unknown spices, a bit of orange and pineapple and just a hint of coffee—though it tasted of the *smell* of coffee more than its taste. Finally there was something that stung in the tiniest way and made his throat feel like he was swallowing liquid fire. The warmth went all the way down into his stomach and spread through his arms and legs all the way to his fingers and toes. Again came the same sensation of being filled with princely power.

They sat down and began the feast. From along the table, all the platters of scrumptious food were passed to Matthew first. He piled his plate high with everything he could manage to fit on it, for he was very hungry. It was certainly a breakfast worth waiting for. As he began eating, he found all the food as delicious as the creamy drink. And whenever his goblet began to get low, one of the servers filled it up again.

"Are these scones made with sugar?" Matthew asked the girl on his right.

"Oh yes, aren't they wonderful. That's why they are so sweet."

"I'm not allowed to eat sugar at home."

"I wasn't either before I came here. But Argon taught me that all things come from the earth and that they have been given us to enjoy and to make us whole as we were meant to be."

"How long have you been here?"

"Oh, ages and ages. This is my home now. I can hardly even remember what it was like before I came here."

"Where is your family?"

"This is my family."

"I mean your real family."

"Oh *them*," said the girl in a tone that wasn't very nice. "Argon has shown me that they were never my *real* family at all—my soul-family. That's why he is helping me to forget all about them. He is helping me forget what they look like, and especially to forget all the things they deceived me into thinking were fun and happy. Argon says I never used to be happy at all. They were just trying to control me. Why else would they refuse to let me have sugar? But I am happy here. I am always happy here. Everyone is happy here."

Matthew did not know what to think about all that. But the next instant one of the servers filled his goblet again.

"Argon wants you to drink," she said.

Matthew glanced down the length of the table. At the far end sat Argon, his own goblet lifted high toward Matthew again. Matthew picked up his own and drank. The moment the fiery, creamy, frothing drink met his lips, gradually everything the girl had said made perfect sense.

When the lavish breakfast was over, Matthew began to think about getting back to his grandmother's and grandfather's house. All the children and animals left the table. Some were clearing away the breakfast things. Others went to their rooms or to chores outside. The large kitchen was alive with the activity of washing and drying dishes and beginning preparations for lunch.

Argon took Matthew outside and led him on a tour of the grounds. Everywhere about him he heard children and animals saying to themselves, *I am happy here…everyone is happy here.*

"I think I should be going back," said Matthew at length. "Thank you very much for the fabulous breakfast."

"You enjoyed it, did you?" asked Argon.

"Oh yes, very much!"

"Don't you want to stay?"

"I have been gone a long time. I ought to be getting home."

"Don't you understand?" said Argon. "You are no longer Matthew Robinson, you are Matthew, Prince of the Forest. This is your home now."

"Thank you very much. But I still think I should go."

"As you wish."

"But may I come back?"

"Of course. Your destiny is here now. Return to me when you are ready to move to the palace and take up your princely duties. In the meantime, I will have someone escort you back. When you are ready to return, have no fear. The way will be shown you. Be sure you tell no one where you have been, or what you have seen and heard. Your mission is secret."

"Why is it a secret?" Matthew asked.

"Because our special wisdom is not for everyone. It takes a special kind of person to be able to drink the Elixir of Wisdom and understand its mysteries. That is why we call this the Center of Enlightenment. This is where eyes are opened to the truth. If anyone else knew you had been here and had begun to see the Secret Wisdom of the Ages, they would be jealous. They would tell you that the secret wisdom is dangerous. Eventually you will be the one to lead them into the secrets, once they come to respect the wisdom I will give you. When your family recognizes you as the prince you are, then it will be time to declare your inheritance openly. Until then it must remain secret."

"Surely I may tell my grandfather. *He* is sure to understand. He is a very wise man. And my Opa."

Argon's brow clouded.

"They above all others you must tell nothing."

"But why?"

"Because your grandfather is jealous of my power."

Matthew did not like to hear his grandfather criticized. He did not believe he could be jealous of anybody. But he did not quite have the courage to defend him against what Argon had said.

"What will I tell them to account for being gone all day?" Matthew asked.

"You have not been gone all day. You will be back in time for their breakfast."

Matthew did not understand how this could be. But he asked no more questions.

"Remember, your mission is secret. No one must know of it."

Matthew was not sure he could find his way home. But Argon summoned a bobcat from somewhere on the grounds, and spoke a few words to her.

"Sheena will lead you back through the woods," he said.

With mixed feelings and odd sensations, Matthew left the palace of Argon and began his return journey north through the western edge of the Forest following Sheena the bobcat. He was never sure whether it was a talking bobcat because it never said a word. It was a very long walk. The minute he saw the edge of the Forest in front of them, the bobcat turned and disappeared. Matthew left the shadows of the field and ran the final few hundred yards across the field.

He was surprised to find Timothy still not dressed. Nobody had missed him at all, though his grandmother did wonder why his appetite at breakfast wasn't quite normal.

He could not help looking at his grandfather differently after that. He was pretty sure that his grandfather noticed the change.

FIVE

The Elixir Does Its Work

Everything looked and felt different to Matthew after that. Nothing seemed as nice as before. He began to wonder why he had been looking forward to coming to his grandmother's and grandfather's for so long. It wasn't any fun now. Timothy was such a nuisance, always wanting to go out and play football or kick the soccer ball around the field. He used to love playing ball. Now such games seemed too juvenile for a *prince*.

"Matthew," said Timothy the next afternoon as they finished lunch, "Let's go outside and play football. I want to try to kick—"

"Oh, go play yourself," said Matthew irritably. "I don't want to."

"Can I show you the doll Grandma gave me, Matthew," said Susanna excitedly. "Would you come up to my room, and—"

"No, I don't care about some stupid old doll," snapped Matthew. "What do you think I am, a girl? Who cares about dolls?"

Susanna looked at her older brother with big eyes of hurt and confusion. She burst into tears and ran to her room. Matthew felt a little bad, but not bad enough to apologize. And as everyone knows, feeling bad about something doesn't matter if you don't apologize.

Finally Matthew went outside. There was his grandfather on his knees in his garden planting a new rose bush.

"Everything all right, Matthew?" he said.

"Sure, why wouldn't it be?"

"You look angry about something."

"Why would I be angry?"

"Timothy didn't look too happy when he came outside with his football a minute ago. His face was red."

"What do I care? He wanted to play and I didn't, that's all. Timothy's a baby."

His grandfather eyed him carefully. Matthew glanced away and walked off.

That evening's supper tasted bland and boring to Matthew. Nothing tasted good anymore. How he longed for another swallow of the creamy drink from the king's feast! He was tired of being at his grandmother's and grandfather's. No one appreciated him here. They didn't treat him like a prince ought be treated. His Opa's stories were no longer interesting. What did his grandfather and Opa think he was anyway, a little kid.

As he lay in bed later that night, he decided that he would go to the palace again.

The next afternoon when no one was looking, Matthew crept across the field and snuck into the Forest at the same place the crow had taken him. He was pretty sure he could find the way on his own. As he went, though he had only been there once, his feet seemed to know exactly which direction to go. Several hours later, he found himself coming out of the Forest. There was the brick building ahead!

Excitedly Matthew broke into a run. He expected everyone to gather round to greet him when they saw he had returned.

A few animals glanced toward him, then went on with what they were doing. The cows and sheep in the field took no notice. As he approached the house, he saw several teenagers kicking a ball. They eyed him with expressions he did not altogether like. Some wore expressions of jealousy, others looked like they considered themselves better than him. No one invited him to join in.

This wasn't at all what he had expected.

He walked to the front door. He hesitated a moment, then opened the door and walked inside. He was relieved to see Argon walking toward him.

"Oh, you're here again finally…good," he said.

"Yes!" replied Matthew excitedly. "I found my way easily."

"Of course you did," said Argon matter-of-factly. "Would you like me to show you your room?"

"My room?"

"You are here to stay?"

"I don't know. I just came for another visit."

"You didn't bring your things?"

"I didn't think of that. I wasn't exactly planning to stay. That is…not yet," said Matthew.

"I thought it was understood—this is your home now," said Argon. "Where else would you be the prince but here? This is the king's palace. Have you forgotten?"

"No, sir. I wasn't thinking about all that."

"You must think about it, Matthew. Tell me, who do you think I am?"

"I don't know," said Matthew a little nervously. "A man…the king?"

"I am far more than a mere mortal," said Argon. "I existed long ago in another world, a world of angels and beings who lived even before the world was made. I was sent here, in the form of a man, to bring light to the Forest, and to the whole world. You have been chosen to leave your past behind and enter into that world of preexistence with me. Light cannot live with darkness. This is light, your former life is darkness. So *now* do you understand—you need to bring whatever you want to have here, and then come to stay. It is the only way for you to be the prince of light."

"You mean leave my family?"

"Of course."

"But they are my family."

"What have they ever done for you? Do *they* treat you like a prince? Or do they make you obey everything they say?"

"Well, yes actually—my parents and grandparents do expect us to obey."

"There, you see—what did I tell you. It is the same story as with all who come here, controlling parents. It is why so many of the children of the Forest come here to live, to be liberated from all that. There is liberation and enlightenment here. You will be much happier. And you will be my right hand man. There has never been a boy with as much promise as you have, Matthew. You may even have your own domain some day. When you are truly liberated from those controlling influences, you will rule over everyone."

"Really!"

"Of course. You are a very clever boy. All you have to do is pay close attention to everything I will teach you, and try to put out of your mind all the falsehoods you learned at home. You will soon be free from your family completely. You will be happy here. Everyone is happy here."

At last Matthew got around to the main reason he had returned. "I thought perhaps I could have some more of that warm drink I had when I was here for breakfast," he said,

"I am afraid the Elixir of Wisdom is only for special occasions," said Argon. "It is not an everyday drink."

As they had been talking, Argon had been leading him upstairs and down a long corridor. He opened a door, and told Matthew to go inside, then left him. Matthew sat down on the bed and thought to himself that his return had turned out a little drearier than he had anticipated. After a few minutes he decided that he might as well go back to his grandparents.

He got up and went to the door. But he was in for a surprise. The door was locked from the outside. He tried the latch again, shook the door a time or two, then went to the window to try its latch.

It was no use. He was locked in.

It must be a mistake, thought Matthew. Why would the prince be given a room with a faulty lock? It was an ordinary looking room, too. Not even as nice as the room he and Timothy were sharing at their grandparents. This was hardly a *prince's* room.

He was just about to start yelling and beating on the door, when the latch turned. In walked Sheena the bobcat.

She paused and looked up with surprise.

"I did not know this room was occupied yet," she said. "I just came in to make some, er, last minute preparations. Excuse me."

The bobcat turned to go. Matthew hurried after her and slipped through the door before it closed behind them.

A low sound came from the bobcat's throat. Whether it was a purr or a growl it was hard to tell. As they came down the stairs into the main lounge, Matthew saw Argon across the room talking to a small group of older children.

As he glanced toward them, a momentary flicker of anger flashed from Argon's eyes. He motioned to the bobcat and the two left the house together.

Wonderful and unusual aromas attracted Matthew's attention. They were coming from the kitchen and reminded him of the elixir he had hoped to taste again. But these were of different fruits and spices. Whatever they were, it smelled delicious!

Matthew wandered about. Still nobody paid much attention to him. He heard noises coming from the large banquet hall and walked toward them into the huge room. Inside he saw the huge long table being set for what looked to be another feast.

This was more like it! he thought. Maybe they were going to celebrate his return after all!

He walked to the head of the table. There sat an empty goblet awaiting filling with the wonderful drink. Unconsciously he began smacking his lips.

A girl a few years older came toward him.

"Remembering your turn at the head of the table?" she said without a smile.

"Yes," said Matthew with wide eyes as he turned toward her. "Is this for another breakfast feast tomorrow morning?"

"No, we are laying the table for tonight's supper banquet."

"Oh, good! I did not think I could wait all night until breakfast! Will this be my place again?"

The girl looked at him with a curious expression.

"*Your* place?" she said.

"Yes. This is where I sat before. Don't you remember—I am the prince...Prince Matthew."

She began to laugh. But the sound wasn't humorous. It was a laughter of mockery.

"You don't think you get to sit there *again*!" she laughed. "You are too funny. You've had your turn."

"You mean this isn't always the prince's place at the table?"

"That's where the new prince or princess sits. Our new guest of honor arrives this afternoon."

"What do you mean, the *new* prince. Argon called *me* the prince."

"Father calls everyone prince and princess."

"*Father*...who do you mean?"

"Father Argon, of course. He is our father and king. We are his princes and princesses."

"Are you his very own daughter?"

"All the girls are his daughters, just like you are his son."

"But I'm not *really* his son. My parents are back at our house in the city. I don't really live in the Forest."

"Your *parents*? You mean before you came here?"

"Yes, of course."

"Once you come here, they aren't your parents anymore. Didn't Father explain all that? They never were your *real* parents. That's why we come here—to meet our soul-father and soul-mother. That's why we are so happy here. I am happy here. Everyone is happy here."

She turned and went on with her work.

Matthew was more confused than ever. But he tried not to show it. He didn't want the girl to laugh at him again.

"Well then," he said, "where *will* I be sitting tonight?"

"*You*?" she said, turning toward him as if she had forgotten he was there. "You won't be sitting anywhere. You don't think *you* will be invited to the feast?"

"I only thought—"

"You will have supper in your room, as do all the new princes and princesses while they are still in training. You won't be invited to another feast until the Wisdom and

Enlightenment has grown stronger inside you. You have to be ready before you will eat again from the secrets of Father Argon's table. It has to grow inside you. You have to learn our father's ways. You have to forget all you learned in your former life."

The girl went about her business with the table, and Matthew wandered outside. All about was the same bustle and activity as before. But after being welcomed and fawned over like a prince when he arrived for his first visit, nobody paid any attention to him now. In the distance, Argon was talking to the bobcat—a little angrily from the looks of it. The bobcat was making low hissing sounds.

He did not intend to ask Argon his questions just now. He didn't appear in too friendly a mood. And he didn't want to go back to that room where they had put him. Even playing ball with his little brother was better than that. He would return to the palace another time and find out more of what was going on.

Disappointedly Matthew began walking slowly back toward the Forest. He had had his heart set on more of that delicious drink. He had thought that he was the prince of this place—the *only* prince. That girl was probably just jealous of him.

As the shadows of the trees closed in around him, Matthew began feeling a strange urge to stay. He *felt* it inside him like the pangs of hunger. It was a rumbling, growling down near his stomach. With every step further into the Forest the feeling grew. Soon it began to get painful. After another few minutes he had a serious stomach ache, like he had gulped down ten green apples. Whenever he glanced briefly back toward Argon's palace, the pain subsided. A time or two he almost changed his mind and turned around and started walking back toward it. Whenever he did, the stomach ache instantly became a warm feeling like he'd had when swallowing the creamy drink.

Back and forth he went, walking a few steps toward his grandparents' house, then turning a few steps back toward Argon's palace. Every time he turned, the peculiar feeling inside him changed. It felt like something was alive inside him making him feel different depending on which direction he went.

It went on for several minutes. He was not behaving at all like the old Matthew. Someone looking at him would have thought he was a mechanical toy going back and forth.

Then something happened that brought Matthew out of his trance. He heard a sound in the trees above him, a familiar sound, the chattering of animals.

Matthew stopped and glanced up.

SIX

The Prairie Dogs Again

What Matthew saw was a furry ball of reddish-brown and another of gray scurrying down the trunk of the tree beside him. All at once the two prairie dogs, Ginger and Spunky were standing in front of him again. They were standing on their hind legs like they were ready to bite him or hit him if he tried to move.

Now the painful sensation in his stomach leapt about inside him worse than ever. It made the next words out of his mouth sound angry.

"What are you doing here?" he said. "Get out of my way."

"The question is what are *you* doing here," retorted Spunky angrily, "so close…to *him?*"

"What are you talking about?" said Matthew. "You're the ones who told me I was supposed to help the king. You said he had a special mission for me. Well I have seen him and now he calls me his prince and his right hand man. So I don't need you anymore."

The two prairie dogs were alarmed at the change in Matthew. They suspected the reason well enough. They had heard of a magic potion the enemy used to entice the children and secure their loyalty. They feared that somehow Matthew had been lured into his camp and might have drunk it. How could Argon have gotten to Matthew so soon? He must have had spies closer than they realized.

"Nip him again, Ginger!" said Spunky. "Maybe you can wake some sense into him."

"It's no use, Spunky," replied Ginger. "If the enemy's potion is inside him, a bite will do no good. Some greater power than we possess will be needed to open his eyes."

As they were talking, Matthew was feeling two sensations at the same time. He was annoyed at the two prairie dogs for being so rude and not treating him like someone important. At the same time he couldn't help being a little worried about what they said. His stomach was hurting worse than ever.

'You've got the wrong king, boy," exclaimed Spunky at length. "How could you have been so stupid? He's no king but a sorcerer. The man you saw is the enemy of the true King! He's just a pretender!"

"What are you talking about?" said Matthew peevishly.

"He is a deceiver and liar," added Ginger. "Do you think a king would live in a run-down house he calls a palace? He possesses dark magic that masquerades as light. He holds in his grip all who are seduced by his promises. We have heard that he has a special drink that he claims gives wisdom. But it puts you in his power. He is using it to lure the Forest children away from their families."

Matthew gulped and a shiver swept through him. But like so many people when they find themselves in trouble, instead of humbly admitting what he had done, he became defensive.

"How do you know where I've been anyway?" he said irritably. "For all you know, I was just out for a walk in the woods."

"Why this part of the woods!" said Spunky.

"I wanted to explore around here, that's all."

"Don't you think we can tell?" rejoined Spunky. "Don't you think it is obvious where you have been?"

"Maybe you're not as smart as you think," rejoined Matthew. "Whoever said prairie dogs were smarter than boys anyway!"

"Just answer one question, then—did he tell you to call him your father?"

"No, he didn't!" answered Matthew defiantly, falling into another mistake that people in trouble do, not realizing that it only digs the hole they are in deeper and makes it harder to get out in the end. He didn't tell the *whole* truth. Yet he tried to pretend to himself that he *exactly* hadn't told a lie.

"Did he give you something to drink!" demanded Spunky.

"It's no use asking," said Ginger. "If he did, he can't tell us the truth anyway. If he drank the potion, the magic inside him would force him to lie. We cannot add lying to the rest. That would only deepen the enemy's power over him."

He turned to Matthew, "Do not answer Spunky's question," he said.

As it fell silent in the wood, a cawing of crows reminded them how close to the enemy's camp they still were.

"Quick, we've got to get deeper into the Forest," said Ginger. "Then we must seek the wisdom of the Wise One. He will know how to deliver the boy from the enemy's power."

Ginger thought a moment.

"Spunky, go for Crynac," he said. "You will be able to move more quickly than I can with the boy. I will take him to the Tall Tree. Bring Crynac there. He will tell us what to do."

Within seconds Spunky had disappeared into the Forest and was gone. Ginger turned back to Matthew.

"All right," he said, "follow me. I will lead you to a safer part of the Forest and to the Tall Tree. There we will meet with the Wise One."

"Who's he?"

"The most noble bird of the Forest, a great white peregrine falcon, the leader of the King's Council."

"I'm not going to any dumb tree or talk to any stupid old falcon," said Matthew.

He turned and stormed off with the prairie dog chattering behind him begging him to change his mind.

The pain in his stomach grew worse and worse the farther from Argon's palace he went. When he got back to his grandmother's and grandfather's, he tried to sneak into the house unnoticed. Luckily no one said anything about where he had gone. He did his best to act normal at supper.

He couldn't sleep that night for the pain in his stomach. His conscience was stinging him, too, for how he treated the prairie dogs and his family. He wasn't himself and he knew it. But the meanness and snippiness just kept coming out of him. He couldn't help it.

Halfway through the night Matthew heard cawing outside. Crows were swirling about the house. He shivered at the sound and tried to ignore it. He knew they were Argon's crows.

Just before dawn, Matthew dozed off. When he awoke Timothy was already up and gone. Suddenly Matthew heard a tapping on the window. He glanced across the room. There was Ginger on the windowsill tapping with his paws.

"Let me in…let me in!" he said.

Matthew got up and went to the window and opened it. Ginger dashed inside.

"I've had a terrible time keeping out of sight of the crows," he said.

"Why are you here?" asked Matthew, less irritably than before. The sleepless night had humbled him a little.

"You've got to listen, you foolish boy," said Ginger. "Because of you, Spunky has been captured. You must help. You have to meet the Wise One."

Guilt bit Matthew hard at the news of Spunky's capture.

"Can I really…do you actually think I can help him?" he said.

"Come to the Tall Tree this afternoon," said Ginger. "You know the way from here. But you must be careful of the crows. They are watching your every move. We will try to distract them. When you see them fly off, make a dash for the Forest and do not stop until you are in the shelter of the Tall Tree. They will not be able to see you. We will come to you there. If we are not there, wait. Spunky's life may depend on it. I cannot force you. But I hope you will."

That morning Matthew was a little nicer to Timothy and Susanna and his grandparents and Opa. He kept an eye on the sky near the Forest the whole time. He heard crows all day and saw them swirling about in the trees at the edge of the Forest.

A little after lunch, as he and Timothy were kicking the soccer ball about, suddenly a huge ruckus erupted near the woods. The crows were swirling about, then flew off in a flurry of black in the direction of Argon's palace. Within seconds the skies were silent.

Matthew ran to Timothy.

"Timothy," he said. "I have to go. There is something very important I must do. I am sorry I have not been very nice to you in the last few days. I will make it up to you and explain everything soon, I promise. But now I must go."

"Where, Matthew?"

"Into the Forest."

"Can I come too?"

"It may be dangerous, Timothy. It is something I must do alone. You stay here and watch over your sister."

The next instant Matthew dashed across the field toward the woods.

He entered the Forest and kept running and running until he was deep amongst the trees. He was relieved to hear no cawing of crows anywhere.

Finally he stopped for a rest. He thought he heard something behind him, but couldn't be sure. The sound hadn't come from above him in the trees but sounded like something soft walking on the Forest floor. As soon as Matthew stopped, so did the sound.

He waited a minute, caught his breath, and continued on.

Wise One of the Forest

Matthew made his way again through the Forest along the same route as when he first encountered the prairie dogs. Many things were going through his mind. So much had changed since then. He had changed, too. He knew it, though he didn't want to admit it. He hadn't been very nice recently.

His stomach ache kept getting worse and worse. He kept thinking that it would get better if he could just get another drink of Argon's elixir. That's what he needed. It would soothe the pain and make it go away.

But after what the prairie dogs said, he didn't know what to believe. That was another reason he needed another drink of Argon's mixture, to give him wisdom so he would stop being confused. If what they said about Spunky was true, he had to try to help him. He didn't *really* think it was his fault. But there was enough of the old Matthew left that he knew he had to try to do something. The whole thing about a conscience is whether we listen to it or not, and do what it tells us. Matthew had been ignoring his conscience a good deal lately. But deciding to do what Ginger had told him and try to help was a huge step in the right direction. When it comes to obeying the conscience, tiny decisions are as important as big ones.

Matthew reached the Tall Tree. No one was there, though he kept hearing what sounded like someone following him.

He sat down and waited. By now he was perfectly miserable. He was tired from the sleepless night and long walk. And the pain in his stomach was almost more than he could bear.

After what seemed hours and hours, but was really only about ten minutes, suddenly a great shadow darkened the Forest floor. It was even darker than the shadows from the trees.

Startled, Matthew looked up to see the enormous wingspan of a great bird whose feathers contained a few shades of brown and black and gray amid a plumage mostly of white. It was descending in a circle toward him. A pang of terror shot through him, for it was a fierce looking bird. At the same moment whatever was in his stomach leapt about and hurt so bad he let out a cry of pain.

His terror at sight of the huge bird only lasted a second. From out of the leaves and branches above him, the red coat of Ginger scampered down the tree just as the great peregrine falcon glided to the ground.

Matthew rose to his feet and stood waiting. By now he had become accustomed to seeing prairie dogs half as big as he was. It was a whole new shock to see this majestic white peregrine falcon standing on its two legs fully as tall as he was himself. The enormous falcon came to rest and stood in front of Matthew. He stared straight into his face with two eyes of the lightest most penetrating gray. Not a feather twitched. His eyes did not blink. For all Matthew could tell, the giant bird might have been stuffed!

"So you are Matthew Robinson, grandson of the fabled Bookman," it said at length. The voice was not at all what Matthew expected. It wasn't a bird voice, scratchy and high, but a calm, soothing, melodic tenor that sounded almost like the falcon was singing. "I am called Crynac," he added. "I understand that we have a problem, and that you are at the center of it."

At last the falcon's neck swiveled in the direction of Ginger who stood beside them.

"How much does he know?" he said.

"Very little, Wise One," replied Ginger. "We had only begun to instruct him when the deception took place."

The falcon's head turned back toward Matthew. "I understand you have been with the Deceiver, the pretender-king who calls himself Argon," he said.

Where Matthew might have been snappy and defensive earlier, the eyes of the peregrine falcon and the authority of his voice, and the fact that he was finally paying a little more attention to his conscience, compelled an honest reply.

"Yes, sir," said Matthew sheepishly.

"What did he tell you?"

"That he was the king of the Forest and that I was the prince."

"And you believed him?"

"I didn't know not to. The prairie dogs told me the King wanted me for a special mission. I thought they were talking about him."

"Please, young man—do not defend yourself. Give me a straightforward answer. Did you believe him?"

Matthew hung his head in embarrassment. "Yes, sir, I guess I did."

"How did you come to meet him?"

"A crow came—a talking crow, you know—came to my grandfather's house and told me the king wanted to see me and to follow him. I thought he was—"

The falcon raised one of his wings as if lifting a finger to stop him.

"I understand. You do not need to say it," he said. "You took him to be a friend of the prairie dogs."

"I'm sorry," said Matthew. "I didn't know."

"*Are* you sorry, Matthew Robinson? Do you mean what you say, or are those words merely to keep from arousing my anger?"

Matthew glanced back and forth between the falcon and the prairie dog.

"I...I think I mean it," he answered after a moment.

"You must be sure," rejoined the falcon. "Much depends on your answer. What depends on it most is your own destiny. But do not answer further for now. The time approaches when you will have to know whether or not you are truly sorry. That moment is not yet. First I must ask you another question, even more important: Did the Deceiver offer you something to drink that smelled more delicious than anything you had imagined in your life?"

Matthew looked down at the ground.

"You must answer me, son. I must have the truth. Many lives depend on it."

Again it was silent for several seconds.

"Yes, sir," Matthew finally answered softly.

"Did you drink it?"

"Yes, sir."

At the words, a great stab of pain shot through Matthew's stomach. He grabbed his side and cried out in agony.

Crynac closed his eyes and sighed deeply. "It is as I feared," he said.

He turned and walked slowly away a few steps, obviously deep in thought. When he turned toward them, he approached Ginger.

"Would that we had Shibnah, Barnabas, and Chebab with us at this momentous hour," he said. "All we had hoped for may now be in jeopardy. If he has been turned to Argon's cause, even his words of regret may count for naught."

"Can nothing be done?" said Ginger.

"There is always hope. But it will be more difficult than any of us imagine, and possibly more painful than the boy can endure."

"Perhaps it is time to summon the Council," said Ginger.

"What about Spunky?" said Matthew before the falcon could reply. "Isn't there some way I can help rescue him, like you said?"

The two turned to face him

"Not as things presently stand," replied the falcon called Crynac. "With Argon's lie inside you, there is nothing you can do to help anyone."

"But please...my stomach hurts dreadfully. It must be from the drink. Is there no way to get its magic out of me?"

"That depends on whether you merely want to be relieved of your discomfort, or whether you believe you did wrong."

Matthew stared back, trying to grasp the meaning of the words. The falcon saw his confusion.

"It may not have been wrong of you to go with the crows," he explained. "You thought they were sent from our King. That was an honest mistake. But when Argon appealed to your pride, he began to suggest that you were more important than you really were. *That* was the moment the lie entered your heart. Your wrong was believing that you were better. We call it thinking too highly of oneself. His magic potion only increased the power of the pride you had already allowed to take root inside your heart. That is

55

the power of Argon's deception—he uses just enough truth to make his victims believe the lie."

Matthew hung his head as he listened. He knew everything the falcon said was true.

"There *is* a way, only *one* way, to break the spell," Crynac went on. "You must do it yourself. The moment has come when you must know, son of Robin—you must *know* if you are truly sorry for believing the lie of pride, or only sorry to be uncomfortable."

"I *am* sorry, Mr. Falcon," said Matthew. "I was wrong to think I was so important. How can I get the magic of the drink out of me?"

"Do not ask unless you are prepared to count the cost," said Crynac. "The cure is far more painful even than what you are feeling now. It is painful beyond belief. Not many have the courage to endure it."

"Please, I want to know."

"Do you have the courage?"

"I don't know. I can try to be brave…if you will help me."

The falcon turned toward the prairie dog. "Perhaps all is not lost yet," he said. "If his heart is as sincere as his words, it may not be too late."

He turned to Matthew. Again he stared deeply into his eyes.

"The only cure that can help you now," he said after a long moment, "is the Sword of Ainran."

A gasp sounded from Ginger. He well knew of the fabled sword and what was its purpose.

"I will help you as far as I am able," said Crynac. "Beyond that, the rest will be up to you. Not many have hearts stout enough to do what the sword requires. That is why so few take up the holy blade. They prefer to keep the lie alive within them. So I ask you again, have you counted the cost?"

"Yes, sir. That is, I think so."

"No one has yet renounced Argon after drinking his magic potion. His ranks continue to swell with the deceived. To denounce him will enrage him. He will unleash all his power to destroy you. Are you prepared to endure it?"

"I don't know. If you and the others help me, I will try to be strong."

"Then you will be strong. We will help you resist him. If you can, it may be that your renunciation of the lie will open the door for many to follow. It may be for the greater good of exactly this purpose that your fall will be turned to good in the end. So again I ask if you are certain."

By this time Matthew really did regret falling prey to the deception. He was genuinely sorry for how he had behaved to his brother and sister, and also for not telling his grandparents what had happened.

"Yes," he said. "I am certain. Tell me what I must do."

The great peregrine falcon closed his eyes. It was silent a long time. At last he opened them and turned to Ginger.

"What will come next I cannot see," he said. "Much will depend on the boy, and what is accomplished on the mountain. I cannot foretell the result. But it is time for him to journey to the precincts of the Garden. There we will see if the King has chosen his prince well. In the meantime, summon the Council. When I return, either alone or with the boy, much will have to be decided."

The Sword of Ainran

Crynac led Matthew far into the depths of the Forest where Matthew had never been before. The journey was long and tiring. No words were spoken between them. They crossed the wide river called Calumia, walked for some time along the banks of a lake where they spent the night, though Matthew did not sleep much. The next morning they went on through a dense undergrowth of what seemed to Matthew like a jungle. He heard the sounds of many strange animals living deep in its tropical rainforest climate. The pain in Matthew's stomach worsened with every step.

Gradually their way steepened as they turned northward until at last they came to the foot of a high range of mountains.

"We are nearly to the western entrance to the Garden of Ainran," said Crynac. "The purging sword sits at the gate. The Sword of Ainran guards this path into the Garden. The way is steep. I would fly you the rest of the way on my back if it was allowed. But the road up this lonely hill is one you must walk yourself. The journey is part of the cure. Are you prepared to continue to the summit where our quest will end?"

"I am very tired, Mr. Falcon," said Matthew. "The pain in my stomach is unbearable. But I want to continue, whatever my fate."

Crynac nodded. Without another word he began to walk up the mountain. Matthew followed.

The way became hard and difficult. No path guided their steps. It was a way not frequently trod by many of his kind.

After what seemed an interminable climb, the summit at last rose before them. They came to a small clearing. At its far end Matthew saw a sheer cliff hundreds of feet high rising toward the sky. All around were jagged rocks and peaks so precipitous there could be no possible way past them. From somewhere nearby he heard the thunder of what must surely be the falls of a mighty river. It was in fact the headwaters of the very river they had crossed the day before. In front of the cliff on the flat plateau sat a conglomeration of stones of diverse sizes and shapes. As they approached, Matthew saw that they were laid out in two long heaps, crossing one another at the center, one slightly longer than the other, perhaps six or eight feet in length. The whole uneven mass was some four to six feet high. Thousands of stones had been thrown one upon the other, obviously by man or beast for some purpose. A few were so huge they must have been dragged by oxen or elephants to the site. Among these were a numberless multitude of smaller stones such that the top of the mound of the two crossing lengths was relatively flat, though bumpy and rough with many protrusions of sharp rock. At the center of the great pile, where the two lengths of stone crossed, a sword of gold and silver rose high against the background of the vertical cliff behind it. The tip of its blade was embedded in the pile of stones, its hilt angled up toward the sun, gold glittering in the light.

Matthew shuddered at the sight.

"Behold the Sword of Ainran," said Crynac. "The time has come, son, for you to take up your destiny. A death awaits you, for you must slay the evil inside you. Are you strong for the task?"

Matthew trembled. "I will try," he said softly.

"You are willing, at least, and that is more important than a thousand empty promises. Let us then do what we came here to do. Even if it should kill you, you will be better off dead than under the rule of Argon's magic."

"Might it really kill me?"

"Of course. What did you think, that it was a toy sword? The Sword of Ainran is a sword of healing. Slaying the evil we have nurtured within ourselves must assuredly end in death—either ours or the annihilation of the evil. There is no other way."

"I do not want it inside me any longer. So I suppose I am ready."

"You are brave and I commend you. Take off your shirt."

Matthew did so.

"Now climb the pile of stones and remove the sword."

Drawing in a final breath for courage, Matthew began to climb up the conglomeration of rocks. He slipped as he went, for the stones were loose. He skinned his knees and shins and hands and finally had to crawl awkwardly while slipping and sliding about. He nearly fainted from the throbbing in his stomach. But he blinked back tears and struggled on. Finally he reached the top of the jagged pile and stood. Ahead of him he now saw that the sword was protruding from a flat white marble slab some four feet square set exactly at the crossing intersection of the two rows of rocks.

"You must lie down on the altar," said Crynac who had flown to the top of the pile and now stood beside the marble slab. "Place the sword at your side."

Matthew took hold of the hilt of the great weapon. A tingle swept through his body. At the same moment a slashing stab in his stomach buckled his knees. He steadied himself, pulled the sword from the hole in the marble that acted as its sheath. It was of great weight. Matthew was just able to hold it. He set it on the slab, laying lengthways across the rough stones. He then lay down beside the sword, the center of his back on the marble slab.

"Cross your hands over your chest and still your soul," said Crynac. "Close your eyes. Feel the depth of your anguish. Remember its cause. The power to do what you must do comes not from strength, but from *yielding* what you think is your strength. To yield is to find life."

Matthew did as he was told. He remembered that he had believed the lie. His sorrow for thinking too highly of himself was great.

It was silent. Crynac waited for the pain to complete its work.

"Now reach out and lay hold of the sword."

Matthew stretched out his hand and grasped the hilt.

"I will show you where the surgery is to take place, my son," said the falcon. With a brief flutter of his great wings, he hopped to Matthew's side. "You must finish the task by your own hand. Take courage. Are you ready?"

"I am ready."

Crynac lifted one leg, held it above Matthew's abdomen, then extended a sharp claw downward.

A sharp sting trembled through Matthew's body as it bit through his flesh. Slowly the claw slit a clean gash across his white skin five inches long. Crynac stepped back, then leapt off the altar. Matthew felt the warmth of his blood flowing out of him, pouring over his stomach and down his side. With it came the foul stench of burned coffee, spoiled milk, and putrefying fruit.

"Take up the sword and plunge it into the wound," said Crynac. "It will probe your depths and lead you to where the battle must take place."

Matthew lifted the sword. With both hands he raised it straight above him, the tip of the blade poised in the air an inch from his stomach. He hesitated with a momentary flinch of terror. The next instant he pulled it straight down.

He cried out in anguish. The blade plunged into the bloody incision of his midsection. A searing heat of fire exploded as the point bore into his flesh. Still flat on his back, Matthew pulled down with all his strength. The blade sliced deeper and deeper through him and into the marble slab on which he lay. At last it disappeared inside his body. Only the hilt remained in his hands. With horror Matthew lifted his head to see blood spewing from him.

He must surely have fainted from the ghastly sight, and from the excruciating white-hot pain, had not a terrible commotion erupted in his depths. It twisted and trembled and buffeted Matthew's body in convulsions. As his frame shook violently, he could not move to escape it. He was pinned to the marble slab by the sword sticking straight through him.

His hands still clutching the hilt, with a mighty effort Matthew now yanked the sword from within him. It came out in a single motion. He tossed the sword aside and it clanked on the stones. Matthew felt himself released from the slab, though his whole frame still shook and trembled. He was being thrown about by some unseen force. There was something inside him! He plunged his right hand deep into the wound. His fingers fell upon the writhing unknown whose fury the sword-blade had waked. With a strong grip he clutched round it and tugged with every ounce of strength that remained.

He had not thought it possible, but the pain inside him mounted to unbelievable anguish. He cried out to keep from fainting, pulling and twisting and heaving at his burden as if he was pulling at his own very heart. He fought on. Slowly, by degrees, whatever was inside him began to yield.

All at once, in a huge final effort, he wrenched from within him a writhing wormlike serpent three inches around. As its head met the open air, with Matthew's bloody fingers around its neck, a horrifying shriek pierced Matthew's ears. Two tongues lashed from the snake's mouth. Long fangs dripping with poison flailed at Matthew's hands and neck. Screeching and twisting with great power, the horrid monstrosity thrashed to free itself from Matthew's grip. Though the pain was intense, Matthew continued to pull with all his might. But the serpent-worm's wildly contorting tail remained buried inside him.

The fierce battle continued. Shrieking with sounds as from hell itself, the viperous fangs spit yellow venom toward Matthew's face. His hands grappling the dread creature below its dangerous head, Matthew gave a final yank of superhuman power. He felt a slippery release inside his depths. The serpent's tail slid from inside him. Instantly, Matthew's pain left him. The entire beast, dripping with Matthew's blood, now writhed about in his hands.

With sudden newfound strength, still clutching the beast round the neck, Matthew jumped to his feet, a true prince of the kingdom in the making now. He held the evil thing in front of his face.

"What is your name, demon!" he shouted.

A tremendous shriek rent the air. The viper's two tongues lashed toward Matthew in a desperate effort to save itself.

"In the name of the true King of the Forest, I demand to know your name!"

A low, earthly guttural sound gurgled from the serpent's throat.

"Tell me!"

A low rumble of hatred growled at him.

Matthew shook the demon-head violently with the strength of the ages. At last came another sound, low, evil, so hideous it could only be from another world, and that from depths where no mortal dares venture.

"I demand that you speak," said Matthew with forceful authority. "I *command* you to speak!"

"I am the Liberator," snarled the snake at last.

Matthew trembled at the word.

The moment it was forced to divulge itself, the serpent's power weakened. Still holding its neck with his left hand, with the other Matthew stooped down and grabbed the sword where it lay. He threw the creature to the ground and with a swift blow sliced off its head, then whacked and smashed with the blade until the grotesque black form lay in a hundred pieces at his feet. A black oozing oily foul-smelling substance stained the marble and all the rocks around it.

Matthew stood back, panting and sweating from the battle. The pain in his stomach was gone. He looked at his bare stomach and chest. No sign of his wound remained. The bloody spots and scrapes from his hands and knees had disappeared. He felt strong and clean. No more blood stained his hands.

His brain cleared and he saw all clearly—his grandfather and grandmother and Opa and Timothy and Susanna and the prairie dogs and the deception he had allowed himself to believe. He fell on his knees and wept in remorse for the thoughts he had allowed himself to think and the rude things he had said to those he loved.

After some time, he stood again. The remains of the creature he had slain and its foul blood were gone. No sign remained on the white marble slab of his own blood. Scattered about the surrounding stones were odd flakes of white. On the marble slab now appeared letters of some strange language, tiny tongues of fire flickering up from them, whose meaning was sealed to him.

Matthew picked up the sword where it lay. With honor and reverence he replaced its blade into its stone sheath at the center of the slab. As it came to rest, the tongues of flame faded away, leaving the strange letters carved an inch deep into the marble.

Slowly Matthew descended the mound of stones. Crynac the falcon stood waiting patiently.

"Did you see?" he said, extending a wing toward the altar of stones. "Your new name is written on the marble slab where you met the enemy and spilled your blood to defeat him."

"I saw figures in what appeared an ancient tongue."

"They were etched in the marble by fire and blood. That is your name now."

"What is my new name?" asked Matthew.

"That is only for you to know, my son. To discover it is your destiny. The Book of Prophecies says, *To him who overcomes, will be given the hidden manna. And his new name will be written on the white stone, and is known only to him who receives it.*"

Crynac turned and led Matthew back down the hill the way they had come.

"You met the enemy bravely, Son of Robin," he said. "And you conquered it. Now you and those you love are in even more danger. We must be vigilant and plan our next moves with care."

"I am very tired, Mr. Crynac," said Matthew. He was hardly able to put one foot in front of the other.

"You have endured a great trial. You will not recover for some time. You will rest and be nourished in due course. But Argon will already know of what you did here. Further attacks upon you will begin almost immediately. Even your present exhaustion may be indication that they have begun. Therefore, we must not delay. The Council awaits."

NINE

Counsel in the Den of Crynac

Before they had gone a great distance, Crynac realized that Matthew would not have strength to complete the journey back to the lake before nightfall. His ordeal had taxed him to the limit of his endurance. He needed to get him to the Tall Tree as quickly as possible, both for rest and safety.

He stopped and looked into Matthew's weary face. If a falcon could have smiled, he would have. As it was, he had to smile with his eyes. "You are tired, my son," he said. "Get on my back. I will fly you the rest of the way. We will get back quickly without having to spend another night away."

Matthew was too tired to argue. He did not even think about the danger. He reached around the falcon's neck, grasped his hands together, and suddenly felt Crynac's wings spreading out beneath him. The next instant they swooped steeply into the air. A momentary flutter of terror as they soared high toward the treetops brought him fully awake. Within minutes he was nearly asleep again. He felt as though he was laying on the softest bed of feathers imaginable, with a warm fragrant breeze sweeping past him, though the falcon's body kept him from the brunt of the wind. Whichever direction he looked, the plume of white swirled and fluffed about him. He was flying above the world in a feathery nest of softest down!

He remembered the words from one of his favorite books:

He peeped through the woven meshes, for he did not dare to look over the top of the nest. The earth was rushing past like a river or sea below him. Trees and water, and green grass hurried away beneath. There was a great roaring, for the wind was dashing like a sea; but at North Wind's back, of course, he felt nothing of it. He was in a perfect calm.

Matthew dozed several times, woke, and dozed again. Somehow he was kept safe and comfortable all the while on Crynac's back, even when he forgot to hold on tight. Because they had to remain below the tops of the trees to stay out of sight of the crows, their course was zig-zaggy through the trees. That kept Matthew from falling asleep altogether.

After a long flight, finally Matthew felt them descending, though not steeply. They slowed and came to light on the branch of an enormous tree. They were nearly as high as the tops of the trees surrounding them. But the branch where Crynac landed was only three-quarters up from the ground to the topmost tip of this giant redwood.

"We have arrived at our destination," said Crynac. He folded his great wings and fluffed them invisibly into his body. Matthew stepped off his back onto the sturdy branch. "I must leave you for a while," said Crynac. "I will fly south and east to make sure we were not followed and to divert any curious eyes that might be about. Argon's crows are devious creatures. You will be in good hands. Trust your guides. You will be blindfolded, but it is for your own safety. I will see you soon."

So saying, he extended his wings again, flapped twice, and was quickly out of sight.

Matthew was only alone a few seconds. Before he had time to think what would come next, a great surging of birds and two monkeys clustered around him. One of the birds, a chickadee, he thought, but it was hard to tell because it was as big as a football, carried the end of a cloth in its beak and began flying around Matthew's head so fast he could hardly keep his eyes on it. Before he knew it, the cloth was fast and tight around his eyes and somehow kept in place at the back of his head.

"Don't worry," said one of the monkeys. "You will be safe. We will guide you."

Its voice was altogether unexpected and unlike anything he had yet heard in the Forest. It was high of pitch but very human and mature-sounding, refined and cultured, like it had been to college. He and a few other monkeys took hold of his hands and led him a few steps along the branch. By now, with the flurry of activity, Matthew had become a little disoriented. He wasn't sure where he was going.

"Step slowly," said the monkey. Matthew felt several monkey hands on both sides of him. Their tiny leathery hands were just like a child's, with busy fingertips moving and flexing every second.

"Duck your head...easy, a little lower...stoop down...now reach out with your right foot...up a little...you will feel a small floor ahead of you—that's it... you may stand again."

Matthew did so and relaxed.

"Now we will descend by ladder," said Matthew's first monkey-guide. "It will be a long climb. Use your hands and your feet. One of us will be above you, one below. No harm will come to you. The way is safe but long."

Matthew could not tell where he was, whether he was in some kind of elaborate tree house, or was climbing down the trunk of the tree. The railings of the ladder were round and slightly bumpy and uneven, like tree branches. The air felt close and still and full of reminders of wood and pitch and dampness and growing things.

The descent was tiring. Just about when he thought he could not keep his hands and feet grasping the ladder any longer, and it was especially hard and a little frightening in the dark, one of the monkeys spoke again.

"You may step off the ladder," he said. "You have reached the bottom. We will leave you now. We must return to our post."

Matthew felt himself handled by more furry paw-hands, and led gently away. Beneath his feet was the soft springy feel of earth. He was relieved no longer to be in the tree tops.

"Come with us, son of Robin," said a kindly voice. Matthew couldn't tell what kind of animal it was, perhaps a squirrel or beaver or raccoon, he guessed by the feel of it at his side. Furry arms and paws continued to guide him along a step at a time.

They walked a good way, turning this direction and that. Matthew had to duck low once or twice and even crawl on his hands and knees once through a tunnel. At last they arrived at a large room. There his blindfold was removed.

Candles burned in sconces around the walls of what looked like a great hall. He was standing on a dirt floor, with a ceiling above that looked like it was made of branches and leaves. He was obviously underground, though it didn't exactly look like a cave, more perhaps like a huge beaver lodge than anything Matthew could imagine.

It was perfectly dry, however. And since Matthew had never been in a beaver lodge any more than you or I have, he really didn't know what one was like, except for what he had read about in books.

He rubbed his eyes and looked about in the thin light to get used to his new surroundings. Then he saw a familiar figure walking toward him. It was Ginger the prairie dog, whom he now considered probably his best friend in the Forest.

"Hello, Matthew," said Ginger. "I am told you have done well."

Matthew smiled a little sheepishly.

"I am sorry for speaking rudely before," he said. "I wasn't myself."

"We know," said Ginger. "All that is past. The future lies before us. It is all we have and we must take it. An important meeting will soon take place. I know you are exhausted. Would you like something to eat and drink while we are waiting, and perhaps a short rest?"

"A drink of water would be very nice," replied Matthew. "And would it be all right for me to lie down for a few minutes?"

"Come with me," said Ginger.

He led Matthew out of the larger room, down a dark narrow corridor, and into a small room. There a bed of moss and leaves was spread with a quilt that looked as if it had been woven with some combination of heather and sheep's wool. In our world such a thing would be impossible, but to Matthew it looked soft and inviting. Matthew also heard a trickling sound. He glanced toward it to see the water of a subterranean spring bubbling out of one of the walls. It flowed out from the side of the room in a tiny waterfall, clear and pure but almost green of hue. It poured without losing a drop into a green marble basin on the floor. Out of this basin the water tumbled to become the most perfectly babbling little brook, winding through a narrow course along the edge of the floor, which remained perfectly dry, and finally out beneath the far wall.

Matthew went to the source and drank deeply from the spout of water. It tasted more delicious than any water in the world. He felt immediately refreshed, and suddenly very, very sleepy. He lay down on the mossy bed, pulled the soft heathery blanket over him. In seconds, with the gentle sound of the healing waters flowing through the room in his ear, he was fast asleep.

When Matthew awoke, he had no idea how much time had passed. He came to himself and gradually remembered where he was. A brief spasm in his abdomen reminded him of the sword and what had taken place on the mountain.

He rose from the bed, which was about the most comfortable bed he had ever lain in, and took another drink from the wall-fountain. Again he felt refreshed. He became aware of voices coming from the big room outside. They were raised in heated discussion. After a few moments, he realized they were talking about him!

Slowly he walked to the door, then stole along the corridor.

The large room of the cave was filled with fifty or more animals of many kinds. At the front of the gathering sat five animals at a table. They were obviously presiding over the meeting. Crynac the falcon, sage of the Forest, occupied the center position. To his right and left sat Ginger the prairie dog and one of the monkeys who had met him at the top of the ladder before he had been blindfolded. Beside them, a red fox sat on one side next to Ginger, and a huge brown bear stood on the other next to the monkey. By now Matthew was getting used to the idea of being surrounded by talking animals, but he did think the bear looked a little fearsome.

"I don't care what he has done," a badger in the crowded room was saying, "the danger is too great. Once he has been in Argon's power, there is no trusting him. He is in the enemy's power forever. Nothing can bring him out of it."

"We cannot allow ourselves to believe that," said a squirrel not far from where Matthew stood listening. "What about the King's promise that the captives will be freed and Argon's rule toppled? Surely it is possible to bring one out from under the spell, even a foolish boy."

Matthew wasn't sure he liked what he was hearing, though he probably deserved it. He slunk a little further back into the shadows.

"But if Badger is right, is it worth the risk?" now said a deer near the front of the gathering.

Nods and murmurs of agreement went round the room.

"What do we have to lose?" said a skunk next to him. "I am a mother and I have already lost two sons. They are both living at that horrible enlightenment place. I have not seen them since they went there. If that man keeps stealing our children, the Forest will be lost anyway. Risk or no risk, I do not see what choice we have. Do any of *you* want to lead us in battle?" she asked, looking around the room.

"We understand your loss, Mrs. Skunk," said a small red bear. "But don't forget the prophecy—when one who has once tasted of the gifts of the Forest, if he falls into the enemy's hands, it is impossible for him to be brought back to sorrow for his deed."

"It cannot be impossible," said a great brown and white St. Bernard dog called Brandy who was one of Crynac's most trusted lieutenants. "If the boy is the King's chosen one, why do we doubt?"

"I never heard He Who Rules say he was the one," growled a wolverine. "All we have is Ginger's word. Perhaps you got it wrong, Ginger."

Heated discussion now spread through the room. It became louder and louder.

"There may be this to consider as well," put in a large gray hare. "What happened may not actually be technically his fault at all. If so, he may not fall under the judgment of the prophecy."

"Who else's fault would it be?" asked a turtle, rising up on its hind legs so as to be heard in the mounting din. "He went into Argon's camp of his own free will. No one forced him. It is clearly his own fault."

"Consider, Turtle," rejoined the hare, "that he was lured to the enemy's camp by treachery. He was told by the prairie dogs that the King needed him. Then the crow came summoning him to a king. What was he to think? How could he have known that there was a false king, or that the crow was not in league with us?"

"The prairie dogs should have given him more information."

A huge ruckus of defense arose from Ginger and some of his friends, especially the other prairie dogs, chipmunks, and squirrels.

"If he is so important a human as to be capable of leading us in battle," insisted the wolverine, "I say he *should* have known, whatever they told him or didn't tell him. Do you expect me to trust my life to one who made such a foolish mistake as to listen to a crow. Everyone knows crows lie through their beaks."

"Perhaps humans don't know," said Mrs. Skunk a little angrily. "We're not all perfect like you, Wolverine!"

"Peace, all of you," finally interrupted Crynac. His voice was calm but unmistakable. He swung his head round in both directions to the other members of the Council. "Would any of the Council speak?" he asked.

"I believe the boy to be true," said Barnabas the Fox.

"On what basis, Barnabas," rejoined Crynac.

"On my judgment of his character according to what you and Ginger have told us. And I think Jumper's point is an astute one. The boy's mistake may not have been rooted in treachery at all."

"Then we have a difficult decision to make," said Crynac. "Before us we have the conflict between what we understood to be the King's choice of the boy, Matthew Robinson, and the prophecy spoken by Redtail the Bear that once having tasted and fallen away, complete faithfulness is thereafter impossible. We can disregard neither word. Therefore, the Council will withdraw to discuss the matter further. In the meantime, son of Robin," he added, looking past the assembly of animals into the shadows of the adjoining corridor to where Matthew stood listening, "I suggest you come in and join us. Allow the assembly to see you for themselves."

A buzz of astonishment, in a tumultuous blend of high and low pitched animal voices, broke out. All heads turned toward Matthew with many expressions on their animal faces. Some showed deference and respect. Others were obviously withholding judgment. Still others eyed him as if he were a traitor in their midst. Most still wondered how a mere boy could lead them against such great odds as they were facing.

"I adjure you all," added Crynac in a voice of command, "in the name of He Who Rules—questions and discussion concerning Matthew's guilt, innocence, or fitness for command are at an end for now. Introduce yourselves. Meet the boy. Tell him of yourselves and the Forest and what we face. But do not question him about his association with Argon. If he chooses to share, he must be free to do so without recrimination."

The five members of the Council rose from the table and disappeared. Matthew walked sheepishly into the room. He was immediately surrounded by a boisterous throng of animals pressing forward to meet him, some more enthusiastic than others.

The Council did not remain away long. As they returned, the room quieted.

"It is the opinion of the Council," said Crynac loudly, "that there is but one way to resolve the conflict before us. That is to consult the Book of the Prophecies."

At mention of the sacred text, a deep hush descended upon the hall.

"Therefore, I will make what haste I can and will fly to the southern gate of the Garden where the Book is kept. We know about the deep magic and the yet deeper magic that saved our sister kingdom from perpetual winter. Now the inheritance of the Forest we are commanded by our forebears to leave our children is threatened. We must discover if any such prophecy is meant to guide *our* way in this present peril. Monkeys, come—I am ready for you to guide me out. Meanwhile, there is food and drink aplenty. Refresh yourselves until my return."

TEN

How Trouble Came to Pellanor

When Crynac was gone, Matthew glanced around nervously.

After hearing the discussion about his visit to Argon's palace, or whatever it actually was, he didn't think the animals liked him very much. He had heard enough to know that the badger, the wolverine, and the turtle were suspicious. But he was surprised to find most of the others warm and friendly. And with Ginger and Barnabas the Fox beside him, along with Jumper the Hare, he soon made many new friends. He was still tired from what he had been through. But the nap and the spring water had helped.

"Where are we, anyway?" asked Matthew after most of the animals had introduced themselves. "Is this an old beaver lodge?"

"I only wish I had lived in such a mansion!" replied one of those present, an aging Beaver known as Widetail.

It was Barnabas the Fox who answered Matthew's question.

"Crynac's den is at the heart of the root system of a great tree," he said. "The location of the tree is kept secret. That is why you were blindfolded…at least for now, until the Council decides what is to be done about you. From above, in the Forest, no one could have any idea where we are."

"How do you get down here? How did *I* get down here?"

"Though it cannot be seen from the outside, the tree's great trunk is partially hollow."

"Is the tree dying?"

"Oh, no—it is as alive as ever," answered the fox. "The hollow trunk is entered where Chebab the Monkey led you, high up the trunk, through a hole just big enough for Crynac to squeeze through. The shaft inside leads all the way down the center of the tree. Because of his size and wings Crynac can't hop about inside it. He must be helped down just as you were. He is pulled up by rope on a little platform, as he was when he left a few minutes ago."

"But why here?" asked Matthew.

"Because Crynac, and all of us on the Council, are in grave danger. A den below the earth is the perfect hiding place. It is invisible from the ground. It is the last place Argon's spies would think to look for a great falcon. The enemy's spies see him flying high above the Forest, but then he disappears. Argon's crows have tried to follow him. But he is able to elude them. He slips into the hole before they know where he has gone. It looks no more suspicious than a woodpecker's house. Crows, you know, are not nearly so clever as falcons."

"What about the big animals?" said Matthew. "And the bear?" he added. He glanced a little nervously toward the huge bear standing on the far side of the room saying nothing. "Surely *you* didn't come down a narrow hole in the tree, Mr. Bear."

The bear did not answer. Again Ginger spoke up.

"There is another entrance through his den," said the prairie dog. "Not even Argon himself would dare venture into the cave guarded by a giant of a bear. When the larger animals are summoned to Crynac's den as now, or when the Council meets, they enter through Shibnah's cave. But it is a long dark walk. Most of the small animals who can climb prefer the tree entrance. But we must be very careful. Sometimes we take hours to gather.

"Who is Argon anyway?" Matthew asked as Mrs. Skunk and several others brought in platters of fruits and nuts and vegetables, with cheeses and bread and butter and several steaming pots of tea to those seated on the dirt floor. "How could he have gained so much power that the whole Forest is threatened?"

A great hubbub arose with everyone talking at once.

"I'm sorry," Matthew laughed. "I'm afraid I didn't understand any of what you said! Maybe you should take turns."

"Our present King," began Ginger, "is of the lineage of our first king Maharba the Great. To understand the threat of Argon, you must understand how the Forest of Pellanor is ruled and where it derives the strength of its life. That strength comes from having always been ruled by the authority of the created order. The Garden has existed, of course, from time beyond reckoning, from the very Beginnings of Beginnings when it was decreed that man should rule the Garden and all the Forest and its animals. That is why there is always a human King ruling over us. All the animals of the Forest know that we were not created to rule ourselves. It is therefore our joy and duty to be loyal to our King.

"The first Kings known in the Annals of the Forest, though their time stretches far back into the mists of antiquity, are Maharba the Great and his son and grandson

Caasi of the Rock and Bocaj Father of Twelve. Their posterity has ruled us through the countless generations since. The final name by which he will be known to posterity has not yet been given to our present King. That is why, like all our Kings until their final names are given, our King is simply known as He Who Rules. Names in Pellanor are determined by the legacy of one's life. One's ultimate name is often not conferred until old age, even sometimes just prior to death.

"There have always been threats to Pellanor, even during the great King's time in generations past. Many battles have been fought against invaders of the Forest who would seize it by force. The Forest is the last place where the created order of rule and authority is preserved through the family and the Legacy of our Kings. That is why this battle is all important. The threat we now face is the most serious in our history."

"Why," said Matthew. "I saw nothing when I was at his palace—well, he *calls* it his palace—"

"Palace, indeed!" huffed Mrs. Skunk. "The imposter!"

Even as she spoke, one of the candles flickered and went out. Everyone looked around a little eerily, as if it was a bad omen to mention Argon at all.

"There are matches up on that ledge on the hearth," said Mrs. Skunk. "One of you tall fellows light that candle."

"I saw nothing that looked like they were preparing for an invasion or anything," said Matthew as Chebab lit the candle again. "It was just like a huge family."

"Exactly!" now said Barnabas the Fox. "They say we foxes are clever and sneaky, but the man Argon is the cleverest of all! That is why we believe that it will take one of his own kind, a human, to defeat him. His weapon is deception and deceit. He is infiltrating the Forest, not with guns and swords and soldiers, but by subterfuge. They are not just *preparing* for battle, the war is underway already. And right now we are losing it."

"I still don't see how he can be so dangerous."

"By luring away the children of the Forest."

"*Luring* them?"

"Yes. It is the Forest children you saw there. Hundreds of them, taken from our own families. He is stealing the strength of our future, the lifeblood that makes Pellanor strong. Many in the past have attempted to conquer the Forest by force. But he has shrewdly undermined the created order. He knows that if the created order of the family is weakened, the life of the Forest will disintegrate. That's how he gained power over his neighboring kingdoms of Shelaharan and Kaldorah. He has been stealing their children for years. Now they are his virtual puppet kingdoms."

"Are those the human children I saw there?"

"Those, as well as the children of his own land of Liwanu and Amotan to the north. All those lands are under his power because they allowed him to destroy their families. Pellanor is his final target."

"Why do human and animal children go to him?"

"You should know better than anyone," replied Ginger. "He deceives them into believing he is something he is not. He pretends everything is wonderful and happy. He promises to give them whatever they want. All the while he is planting seeds of dissatisfaction about their own families. He does it so subtly they do not even realize they are being manipulated against their parents. He calls it liberation and enlightenment, but it is actually rebellion against the created order which rules all creation. Most of the children do not have the strength you did to escape and to stand against his Great Lie."

"What is his Great Lie?" asked Matthew.

"The lie of *I-Am-Better*," said the wolverine, speaking angrily again, but not toward Matthew. "He believes that he is better than other men. They say he thinks himself a prophet. A prophet! Have you ever heard the like of it? He feeds the lie of *I-Am-Better* to those who come to him. It gives him power over them."

"I still do not see why," said Matthew.

"Because down inside everyone wants to believe it," said Barnabas the Fox. "He tells them what they want to hear. He pampers and indulges their selfishness. He tells them that they *are* better than everyone else, better than their friends, better than their parents, better than their brothers and sisters. There are even stories that he tells them they are all actually angels! They believe it because they *want* to believe it."

"I am afraid he does tell them that," said Matthew. "I heard him say it himself. But where did he come from?" Matthew asked, glancing about the room. "Surely he is not part of the Forest or he wouldn't try to ruin it like this."

"Argon is a usurper from the neighboring country of Liwanu to the south," said the turtle. "He and his so-called wife Dezreall masquerade as perfect parents. They invite children to visit. They entice them with sweets and devious foods. But once they drink the magic potion, the Liberator demon is planted in their hearts. It is exactly the strategy they used to rise to power in their own lands. We saw the threat but had no idea their schemes would work here in Pellanor. We thought his lies would only work on human children. We were not prepared for how they managed to infiltrate our families, too. Many of those in this room have not seen their children in more than a year."

A rumble spread about, with sad and angry comments and nodding heads. A few of the mothers dabbed their eyes with the backs of furry paws.

"Who is Dezreall?" said Matthew. "I saw no woman when I was there."

"She was there," said Ginger. "She is queen of Amotan to the north. If you ask me, she is the real ruler of the rebellion."

"Why doesn't your King put a stop to it?" asked Matthew. "Why doesn't he march in and destroy the place?"

"It is not so easy," replied Barnabas. "Our King's power is sustained by the family. When children leave us, it slowly drains hope from the Forest. The King's power, too, has been diminished. The deception can only be undone from within, by children choosing to leave and renouncing the lie. That renunciation cannot be *forced*, it must be *chosen*. That is why you may be the key to victory. You are the first to come out. If we can get more to renounce Argon and Dezreall as frauds, their power will unravel. We have to wake the children in the midst of the deception. But that is not easily done once the potion is inside them."

"To make matters worse," Ginger went on, "He Who Rules was called away some time ago. He has been gone a long time."

"Called away—by whom?" asked Matthew.

"By the King of another land to which he is linked by mutual alliance. During his absence, Argon and Dezreall have stepped up their efforts."

"You say they are husband and wife?"

A snort sounded. All eyes turned again to the wolverine. "So they call themselves," he growled. "But there are dark secrets involved. I have heard rumors. If the truth were known, the whole thing may not be a legal marriage at all according to the ancient law of the Book."

"Why do they want other people's children around them?"

"The family is the strength of the Forest," said Ginger. "With even one member gone, a family is no longer whole. Its unity has been weakened. This is Argon's treachery. He and that Jezebel target children in their most vulnerable years by sowing seeds of alienation."

A sad expression came over Matthew's face. "That is exactly what he did with me," he said, nodding slowly. "He told me my parents didn't really understand me. He kept saying that I was wise and mature and had the right to be treated as if I were a grown-up. I have the best parents in the world. But after drinking that horrid elixir, I began to forget. I cannot imagine that I was so stupid as to believe him."

"That is the power of the Great Lie," said Ginger. "There is no greater evil than turning a son or daughter against his parents. It is a cunning scheme. If they can unmake the unity of enough families, the fabric of Pellanor will disintegrate."

"They will have much to answer for when the King's retribution is meted out against them," said Mrs. Skunk. "What kind of woman steal's the affection of another mother's child. I may never see my own grandchildren. It is all I can do not to hate her."

"Keep faith, Mrs. Skunk," said Barnabas. "We do not yet see to the end of it."

"That is why we believe you have been sent," said Ginger. "I told you that the first day I met you. Time is short. The battle approaches."

ELEVEN

Revelation From the Book

The discussion had been so lively that they hardly noticed as Chebab and his cohort of monkeys pranced with lively step into the room. Crynac was following them.

The room grew silent as the great falcon came into their midst. The other four members of the Council rose—though the bear had remained standing and silent throughout—and again took their places at the table with Crynac in front of the gathering. The room waited for Crynac's report.

"I have been to the mountain," he began. "I have consulted the Book of Prophecies at the southern gate. Among the most ancient of those concerning this time when the unity of the Forest is threatened, I discovered words that may point the way out of our dilemma. The first of the prophecies, the Book of Origins, speaks of the perfection of the Forest and the Garden, of the waters of the four rivers, and of the originating principle of man's rule. But the Book of Second Things foretells that our Kings will neither be perfect men nor perfect Kings, for the race of men is an imperfect race. Nevertheless, they have been chosen to rule us. We live with this imperfection daily and all know it well. Pellanor is surrounded by nations of men who abandoned their founding principles generations ago in order to seek their own ends. It has only been by the faithfulness of our Legacy of Kings that the Forest has preserved its purity from the surrounding stain of man's greed. However, the Book foretells a time when a grave threat will come to our own succession of rule, when the heir himself will succumb for a time to the Lie, and the very Legacy of Kings will hang in the balance. I believe that time is now. The Book speaks of a boy prince whose rule will be jeopardized during a season when the Great Lie will threaten the world and will attempt to undo the perfection of origins, even in the Forest. But I also discovered what I believe points to final victory after that season of peril. It speaks, however, of a remedy I had not expected. Hear the word of the Book:

When treachery stains the child king fair,
   and hope in the land sinks to despair,
Night may yet turn to day
      if by his hand the dragon he slay,
         and has courage in battle to lead the way.
After drinking of waters that from Ainran flow,
      he shall rise from the Garden to strike the blow
that will end the deceit.

      Thus, another such fall he will never repeat,
         but with his own sword shall the usurper defeat."

"You are not suggesting, Crynac," began Chebab, "...that the boy be taken *into the Garden*?"

"I am only repeating to you the words of the ancient prophecy," replied the falcon. "It has long been foretold that a man-child would be sent to lead us in Pellanor's darkest hour. We had no idea that the fulfillment might come in the King's absence, nor that we of the Council would have to face such momentous decisions on our own.

Neither did we anticipate that he would be lured into Argon's power, nor that—"

Suddenly a monkey ran into their midst from the tunnel.

"Silence everyone!" he exclaimed in an imperative whisper. "Many crows are swirling above! Their hearing is keen—not a sound!"

The room went dead quiet. Instantly they heard the obnoxious cawing echoing faintly down through the tunnel.

With a motion of his wing, Crynac summoned a fleet of jays, woodpeckers, and cardinals. A great flurry raised a brief windiness throughout the room They clustered together, hovering in front of the falcon. Then they flew off and disappeared.

"Extinguish the candles," whispered Crynac softly, "just in case."

Again the room, now in blackness, fell silent. A minute or two later, a great squawking and tapping and chirping echoed through the tunnel from above them.

"That should convince Argon's spies that they have found nothing but a hole in a tree," said Crynac. "Our jay friends will make enough noise that we will not be heard. They will drive them away if they get close. You may light a few of the candles again.

"Let this be a warning to us all," Crynac continued when the room was dimly lit. "As careful as I thought I was, I was not careful enough. Somehow they picked up my trail. Our vigilance must become greater than ever. Now, as I said, we did not anticipate that young Matthew would encounter Argon face to face before we could warn him, nor that he would be required to plunge the Holy Sword of Ainran into his own flesh. These have come as surprises to us. But with the future of Pellanor at stake, can we cling to our former expectations? Ancient prophecies often require the light of new times to be understood in their fullness. There may be more surprises ahead."

"What is your opinion, Wise One? Speak, and we will heed the King's wisdom spoken through his oracle."

Heads turned with some surprise to see Randon the Wolverine, not always known for being cooperative, standing and facing Crynac. He gave a slight bow of respect, then sat down.

"Thank you, Randon," said Crynac after a moment. "I can only speak what I see. I do not claim infallibility of vision, though I hope my sight is clear as far as it does see. Thus, it may well be that the time long foretold is at hand."

"When will He Who Rules return?" asked a sparrow.

"Fitting that you should put that question to me, Silverwing," said Crynac. "Your own cousin Fleetwing, who accompanied the King on his journey, came to me on the mountain. He has been on the wing many days. He had just arrived with a message from He Who Rules. The King's return is eminent. His delay has been unavoidable and will be turned to the good in the end. But his time is not yet. Until then, our instructions are to persevere, and to prepare the Son of Robin for what will be required of him."

A raccoon who had not yet spoken rose from their midst.

"I do not mean to doubt your judgment, Wise One," he said. "But I must voice a grave concern about the sanctity of the Garden. If there is the slightest chance of its location being discovered by the enemy, we would be undone. I speak not in doubt of the boy's sincerity. The fact is, however, he is not one of us. He is not of the Forest. Can we risk it?"

A murmur of discussion spread through the gathering.

"You raise a legitimate concern, Gideon," nodded Crynac. "I have considered the question well. Henceforth, all we do involves risk. There will be no easily won salvation of all we hold dear. Risk is the price of battle. If we have heard the King's messenger aright, then we must prepare the boy to lead us."

"But we all know the command," said Widetail the Beaver. "None from outside the Forest is to know the pass through the mountains to the pool. The danger of revealing its location is too great."

"It may be that the risk is too great if we do not get him to the pool," rejoined outspoken Mrs. Skunk. "He is the one sent to rescue our children. He must be at full strength. How else but by drinking the sacred waters?"

"He will have to be strong," said Whitetail the Deer.

"Can he *ever* be strong enough?" rejoined Badger.

The falcon raised his great wings to silence the debate.

"It matters not if he *is* strong enough," said Crynac. "He *will* be strong enough when the time comes. Of that we may be assured. He Who Rules has chosen him. That is all we need know. I believe that we can rest in the assurance that only those with eyes to see will be capable of seeing. It may be time that we put our trust in the ancient proverb. If the boy is not truly one of us, he will see nothing at all."

He paused. The others waited.

"It is my opinion that the boy has fought the battle bravely and done what few have the courage to do, become the executioner of their own deepest demons. But the effect of the serpent's poison remains. The word is true that the evil worm dyeth not except by fire and water. He has endured the fire of Ainran's sword and spilled his own blood in executing the demon. But he will not recover fully from its effects without drinking from the Pool of Ainran. And now we also have the ancient prophecy from the Book confirming that the waters will not only give him the strength needed to defeat the foe, but also to prevent another fall. I believe the prophecy lays to rest the question whether we may trust him. I believe we *must* trust him. Our way is to take him to the sacred pool. But I will not make such a decision myself. It is time for the Council to speak. Is the son of Robin to be taken to the Garden to drink from the Pool of Ainran?"

Again Crynac paused.

"Who casts their choice with the *Ayes*?" he said at length.

Slowly all four on both sides of Crynac raised their paws.

TWELVE

To the Gate

The rest of that night Matthew remained in the den of Crynac, sleeping soundly on the bed of moss and leaves, covered by the blanket of heather and wool with the healing sound of water in his brain. When he awoke he felt more rested than he had for days.

Again he heard voices in the large room. He got up and went to investigate.

"Ah, Matthew, my boy," said Crynac as he walked in. "Did you sleep well?"

"Yes, sir...uh, Mr. Crynac," replied Matthew with a smile. "Very well, in fact. I feel ever so much better."

Matthew saw that all the others from the previous night's meeting were gone. Only Ginger the prairie dog, Barnabas the Fox, Chebab the Monkey, and Shibnah the Bear, who still had not spoken, remained in the underground den.

"Good," said Crynac. "As you see, the five of us are here to accompany you to the Garden. Mrs. Skunk has prepared us provisions, although packing food for a peregrine falcon, a bear with a voracious appetite, a prairie dog, a fox, a monkey, and a boy," he added, chuckling, " — let me just say I am extremely curious what she has found that will satisfy all our tastes! But as you see, there remains much left from last night. So eat heartily now, son of Robin. I cannot guarantee what manner of food will await you in the days ahead. After breakfast we will set out for the High Country."

By now of course Matthew had lost all track of time. It could have been midnight or a bright sunny afternoon, or a dreary rainy morning for all he knew. And whether it had been a few hours, or several days, since he had left Timothy in the field at his grandparents', that he didn't know either. He had a vague idea that they were probably worried about him. Somehow he also had the feeling that Crynac was wise enough to know all about that. So he was pretty sure it would come right in the end.

When they were ready, Chebab, Ginger, and Crynac led Matthew to the hollow tunnel up the center of the tree. Several of Chebab's fellow monkeys were on hand to wield the ropes and pulleys and hoist the platform to lift Matthew and Crynac through the center of the tree. Ginger disappeared up the vertical shaft ahead of them, for of course *he* needed no help climbing through a tree! Meanwhile, Shibnah and Barnabas left Crynac's den through the long tunnel back to Shibhah's cave. This time they did not blindfold Matthew. He knew that they were climbing up inside the Tall Tree where he had first met the prairie dogs.

When Matthew emerged back out of the tree-tunnel into the open air, on the same branch where Crynac had landed with him earlier, he saw that the sun was just getting ready to rise in the east. It was a bright, warm, sunny dawn — the perfect time to begin a journey. However, he still wasn't sure what day it actually was—a day after he'd last seen Timothy, or two days, maybe even three.

Crynac told him to climb onto his back. Once more Matthew was carried up into the treetops. They glided silently through the chilly morning air. The flight this time wasn't nearly so long. In five or ten minutes he felt their descent. They landed in a thick, dense, dark part of the wood where it looked like the sun never reached the ground.

"We will wait for the others here," said Crynac.

It didn't take long for Chebab, who had come through the trees, and Ginger, who had run along the ground, to arrive. But it was an hour or more before they finally heard Shibnah tramping through the underbrush. Barnabas ran up ahead of him.

After a rest and drinks of water, and some discussion between the four speaking members of the Council about the best route to take, they set out.

Most of the way for the rest of the morning took them though thick Forest. Matthew knew the sun was shining overhead because it began to brighten and warm up. But down on the Forest floor it remained damp and chilly. They had to keep out of sight as much as possible. Whenever the trees thinned, or when they came to an occasional meadow, they slowed, listened intently, and proceeded *very* quietly one at a time. Matthew thought he heard sounds in the treetops, though faintly, even sometimes when they were in the open. Occasionally he glanced up, but saw nothing.

"Are you worried that we are being followed, son of Robin," said Crynac.

"It seems I hear birds above us," replied Matthew.

"You are keener of hearing than I realized," said Crynac. "That is a good sign. Already you are developing the hearing of a true child of the Forest. We shall only hope that your *seeing* progresses as quickly. You are right, we *are* being followed. Silverwing has a fleet of sparrows, along with a host of finches, chickadees, and cardinals that are surveying the Forest ahead and behind. We will know if a crow comes within a mile of us."

"And Jumper and Randon are leading a ground troop of squirrels, chipmunks, mice, hedgehogs, badgers, small dogs, rats, raccoons, coyotes, wolverines, and possums," added Ginger. "We are completely surrounded by an invisible guard should the slightest danger approach."

"Won't all that activity make Argon's spies suspicious?" asked Matthew.

"You are beginning to think like a commander!" said Crynac. "If you *were* our commander, then—which you may be before long—what strategy would you employ under the circumstances?"

"I don't know," replied Matthew. "Perhaps a diversion of some kind, to trick them into focusing their attention someplace else."

"Well done!" said Crynac. "That is the very strategy."

"That reminds me of something I wanted to ask," said Matthew. "When I left my grandfather's house, I knew crows were watching me. But suddenly they all disappeared. What happened?"

"As you say—a diversion. I flew up close amongst them with a great flurry and flapping of my wings. They hate me but they are also terrified of me. I pretended to be frightened, as if I had come upon them by accident. Then I flew off south. They immediately followed me, thinking I was up to something. That allowed you to make your dash into the trees unseen."

"Is something like that going on now?" asked Matthew.

"It is indeed. Shibnah's brother, who is even taller than Shibnah, is leading a band of large animals to the south through Sycamore Grove. They set out several hours before we did and are marching straight south toward Argon's

Center of Enlightenment. All the jays are with them, and as you know jays can make a terrible racket. They will have been seen long before now. I have no doubt that Argon is trembling in his private room, Dezreall soothing him with brandy. They have no idea where lies the true battle line for the Forest. They probably think they are under attack. By the time he realizes Beathnah and his leopards and elephants and tigers and horses and our large dogs are but a ruse, we will be safely inside the cover of the Garden, and invisible to any horde of ten thousand crows."

"*Invisible*—how will we be invisible?"

"Did you not tell him of the Garden, Ginger?" said Crynac, glancing behind as he and Matthew walked along together.

"There has been no occasion to do so," replied Ginger. "And I was not certain that I should divulge—"

"Ah yes, of course. I see. Perhaps you should tell him now. I believe the season for secrets is past. While you do so, I will consult briefly with our sparrow eyes above."

So saying, Crynac extended his wings and soared aloft. Quickly he disappeared amongst the trees. As they continued on, Ginger and Barnabas drew alongside Matthew.

"At the heart of the Forest," began Ginger, "in a protected location in the eastern High Country, well guarded—you will meet one of the guards soon—flourishes an enormous Garden. It extends for miles and miles surrounded by mountain peaks the like of which you have never seen. It is full of lush meadows and streams, snow-capped peaks, glaciers and blue ice-caves leading great distances beneath the mountains, thundering waterfalls so high you cannot imagine them. To call it a garden gives a wrong impression. It is an entire land overlooking Pellanor from the east. It has been called The Garden from time immemorial, even though it is a country all its own. Its soil and waters are more fruitful than any on earth. Whatever grows there flourishes with abundance. It is luxuriant with every imaginable type of growing thing—trees and fruits and vines and all kinds of food the ground is able to produce. In the center sits the palace of the King—Sogol Pell Lealnor. From its throne have reigned the Kings of the Forest since it was constructed during the time of Maharba the Great."

"It sounds like a wonderful place. But how can it be hidden if it is such a big country?"

"It can only be seen after one enters it. And no one can enter it until it is seen."

"That sounds like a riddle," laughed Matthew.

"Much of truth seems like a riddle to those on the outside. To see is to understand. To understand is to see. An eternal magic has been breathed into the air of the Garden. It is the mystery of the Creator, the magic of Ainran. To breathe its air is to be filled with the energy and Life of the Ages. All those who sit on the King's Council are required to spend seven nights and seven days at Sogol Pell Lealnor every year, to renew their strength and fortify their wisdom for the challenges they face.

"Spread out below the magnificent marble towers of Sogol Pell Lealnor, a pool of crystal clear cold water of purest emerald green bubbles up from infinite depths. It is more than a mere pool, it is a lake a mile across in one direction and half of that in the other. This is the Pool of Ainran. It is where your destiny is now leading you."

"What is it like to be there?" asked Matthew.

"What is it like?" repeated Ginger. "It is to be more *alive* than you have ever felt in your life. At the middle of the Pool rises a small island known as the Center of Centers. Out of its rich soil grows the One Tree whose roots extend into the depths of the earth itself. It is said to be the oldest living thing in our kingdom.

"Surrounding the Pool of Ainran steep slopes rise all round, out of which open four canyons. Through them flow the four rivers that nourish all the corners of the Forest. From them branch multitudes of streams, brooks, rivulets, underground streams, and springs. You drank from one of these in Crynac's den. The Pool of Ainran is continually replenished with *living* water, constantly bubbling up, flowing out and down the rivers and into all its streams. Legend says that the waters that flow from the Pool of Ainran give eternal life and health."

"I did feel an amazing surge of energy after drinking the water last night," said Matthew. "But who is Ainran?"

"It is not a who, but a place," answered Barnabas, who had been listening to Ginger's account. "It is a sacred land whence flow the waters that feed the pool and sustain the One Tree. Legend says that the land where the waters originate was created first, and that the waters of the Pool thus contain the primary source of power from which all the Forest derives its life. The name of that land is not spoken often in Pellanor, and always with great reverence."

"Where do the rivers go after leaving the Forest?" asked Matthew."

"They once watered the four neighboring countries beyond our borders," answered Barnabas. "But after those lands were taken over by rulers who did not understand the Truths of Foundations, the rivers dried up. The waters are only for those who understand the source of their life. The rivers now disappear underground and return to the springs of Ainran whence they came. Liwanu, Amotan, Shelaharan, and Kaldorah are now parched and dry and perpetually threatened by drought."

"I don't understand how any of this will make us invisible," said Matthew.

"The location of the Garden is miraculously protected by the Magic of Ainran," replied Ginger. "Though Argon's crows may fly over it, they see nothing of the Garden, the Pool, or the glistening white and gold turrets of Sogol Pell Lealnor. Only those meant to see can see. Argon knows of it, though not the location. Dezreall found out about the existence by deep deception years ago. We believe it is her design to use the manipulation of the children to somehow discover the entrance into the Garden."

"Once we get into the Garden, will we be safe?" asked Matthew.

"That is true," replied Barnabas. "Argon will not know where we are. But the rest of the Forest will still be in danger. We cannot hide behind the shield of invisibility longer than needed for you to drink from the Waters of Wholeness."

"What would happen if they did find the Garden?"

"It would be the end of Pellanor—at least as we know it. No doubt machinery would rumble in. There would soon be roads and dams and railroads and cars and noise and smoke and cities and loud music. They would *civilize* the Forest, I think that is the word you humans use, with all the modernism of the Cities of the West. They covet the Garden and its eternal waters. Their ultimate goal is to control them and divert the rivers back to their own lands, and at the same time control the flow to Shelaharan and Kaldorah by a series of dams in the mountain canyons. But they are fools to think the waters of Ainran can be dammed or stored or sold. They are not tame waters. They are manna-waters, to give life, not to be used for selfish gain."

Crynac returned with the report that no danger had yet been seen from the air. As planned, the enemy's attention had been diverted far to the south. Argon's entire company of crows was following Beathnah's diversionary force as they made their way toward Argon's compound.

About mid-afternoon they reached the shores of the greatest of all the Forest rivers, the Western River of

Calumia. It was wide and deep and flowing rapidly and looked to Matthew impossible to cross. Downstream they could hear the sounds of the Rapids of Calumia. Without a moment's hesitation, Barnabas the fox leapt on Shibnah's back and the great bear plunged into the flow and began to swim across.

"On my back again, Matthew," said Crynac.

In less than two minutes, Matthew was deposited safely on the far shore. Crynac returned for two more flights with Ginger and Chebab on his back. He glided in for the last time just as Shibnah and Barnabas were climbing up the bank and shaking themselves off.

By late afternoon Matthew was very tired. He was also feeling a slight pain in his abdomen. Animals never seemed to get tired, he thought, but he sure was. They crossed the central highlands quickly because it had less tree cover and was more exposed. Crynac carried Matthew across on his back faster than they had yet flown. Matthew felt like he was hanging onto the top of an airplane! The others ran for an hour at top speed until they were safely again under the cover of trees and approaching the bank of the Southern River as it flowed south out of the mountains. At first sight, it looked to Matthew like an ordinary river, except perhaps that the water was a little greener than you usually see, as was the Calumia. They turned north and followed it upstream the rest of the day. Their way steepened steadily as the water below became more white and turbulent.

The shadows of late afternoon slowly lengthened around them. They were trudging up a steep climb. Far below the river was nearly all rapids now, with gorges and waterfalls around every bend. It was one of the loveliest places Matthew had ever seen. Ferns grew down to the water's edge. Wild Forest flowers were scattered about their feet. They weren't exactly following a path, yet the five knew exactly where they were going.

Matthew was relieved when Crynac announced that they were nearly to the end of their first day's journey.

"We will be staying the night at the den of Shibhah's and Beathnah's cousin, Miss Fernduddle. Lead the way, Shibhah."

In less than five minutes, Shibnah suddenly turned to his left away from the riverbank where they had been walking. He scuddled his way up the steep hill. Barnabas and Chebab and Ginger had no trouble. They scampered up after him. But Matthew and Crynac could hardly keep up through the thick bushes and undergrowth. Ahead Matthew saw Shibnah crouch down on all fours and suddenly vanish into the side of the hill. Just as quickly Barnabas, then Chebab, and finally Ginger all disappeared from sight. When Matthew got to the same place, he saw a hole in the bank, hidden by bushes and branches. He got down on his hands and knees and crawled in. Crynac followed.

It was dark and damp and smelled earthy. Matthew crawled along until gradually he saw light ahead. In another few seconds he emerged into a large cave dug into the side of the mountain. There were the others, shaking dirt from their coats and standing in the light of several candles and a cheery blaze in the fireplace.

"Welcome, welcome!' said a woman's voice—a woman *bear* that is. Matthew was still looking around when a short stout bear not half as big as Shibnah waddled toward him. "And is this the human you are taking to the mountains! Welcome to you, man-child, I am Fernduddle."

"Hello," said Matthew. "My name is Matthew."

"That's fine, just fine…capital, capital. Now what would you like to drink? Shibnah, be a good fellow and set chairs for everyone, though I don't suppose the rest of you need chairs. But get one for the boy. We don't want *him* sitting on the ground. He has no fur."

Shibhah obeyed, a little timidly it seemed, as if he was a boy being bossed about by his mother. Matthew thought it funny for anyone, even another bear, to order around someone as big as Shibhah. Maybe she was his *older* cousin. He did think he saw a faint family resemblance.

"Poor Shibnah," said the talkative Miss Fernduddle, lowering her voice as Shibnah disappeared into another part of the cave. "He is not so strong as he appears. The reminder that his cub is not with him tears at his tender bear-heart. Not a moment goes by that he isn't thinking about his little Dubpah. There was so much he wanted to do with him, and teach him of the Forest, places he wanted to take him, secret troves of honey he wanted to show him. You will scarcely believe this, but I once came upon him weeping! Big hulking Shibnah. Inside his heart is breaking for his son. I fear for that evil Dezreall if he ever gets his paws on her!"

"Is that why he never says anything?" asked Matthew.

"He vowed not to speak until his son is freed from the clutches of that woman," nodded Miss Fernduddle, "but do not say a word about—"

Just then Shibnah came back into the room. She quickly raised a paw to her mouth and said no more.

They were off early the next morning, but not before Miss Fernduddle had made them a bigger breakfast even than Shibnah could finish, with pancakes (with lots of honey and butter) and eggs and fish and good strong tea and coffee to keep up their energy.

"Now you be sure to stop by on your way back down," she said as they thanked her for her hospitality. "I will have the table spread waiting for you!"

They set out again high above the bank of the river and followed its course ever higher into the mountains.

The way was even steeper than before. By noon, perilous mountains rose on all sides. It didn't seem to

Matthew that there could possibly be a way through them. Still they climbed, with the sound of thundering water plummeting down beside them.

At last they came to a small plateau. Ahead Matthew saw the sheer rock of a great cliff face very much like what he had seen rising up behind the stone altar of the Sword of Ainran. The way in front seemed to come to an end. Nothing but cliff lay ahead. There appeared no way through it.

A thundering waterfall poured down through a gap in the mountain lower down and to their right, gushing out in a torrent of pure green and white. They would certainly never pass *that* way. They would be battered to bits if they tried to get through the river gorge.

"We have come to the southern gate to the Garden," said Crynac, "the Gate of the Book."

"I see no gate, no way through the cliff," said Matthew. "Where will we possibly go?"

The others were eyeing him closely. Matthew did not know it, but he was about to face his first major test since they had set out on this journey. The others, you see, were not certain that some tiny bit of Argon's elixir was not still inside him. They had taken a great risk by telling him about the Garden of Ainran. It was an even greater risk bringing him to the gate. But they had to be certain beyond any doubt that he was the one He Who Rules had chosen to lead them. There was only one way to be *absolutely* sure. They had to test his eyesight. They needed to find out if he could *see* with the eyes that only obedience could open. If the magic cloak of invisibility prevented his seeing, they would know a seed of the Liberator's lie was still alive within him.

It may not seem very nice that they would test him that way. But the future of Pellanor was at stake. They had to know if he had eyes to see. You have to remember that none of them had known Matthew more than a few days. That is not long to know all there is to know about someone.

So now the other five waited a little nervously. The moment of truth was at hand. Would the boy they had brought this far truly *see*?

They studied the expression on his face as he stared at the blank face of stone in front of them.

"Look very closely, son of Robin," said Crynac. "Sometimes when it seems a path is completely blocked, the way is not as closed as it looks. There are solutions through most impasses that we do not observe at first glance. Are you *certain* you do not see a way through the wall of stone?"

Matthew squinted slightly.

"I think you may be right," he said slowly. "It seems that perhaps I see a faint vertical line in the rock face that may be caused by a difference in depth...yes, a portion of the cliff on the right is set back further than that on the left. Perhaps there is a way through that gap."

"Well done, son of Robin!" exclaimed Crynac. "You lead us to it, and we will soon know if your sight has seen truly."

Matthew led out across the bare plateau. As they approached the cliff, he saw that indeed there was an indentation in the set-back of the wall. They drew closer yet. A narrow vertical shaft, invisible from where they had been standing, suddenly appeared to their left. Matthew turned into it, and disappeared into the sheer rock face. Two more turns to the right and again left, high walls of stone on each side, took him the rest of the way. Though the narrow pass was completely barred to view from a hundred feet away, he had walked straight through the cliff!

The moment he was through it, with the others following, the way widened again. Matthew saw a quaint little guardhouse in front of them. The next instant he saw the strangest looking creature walk out of it and approach him with its hand in the air. Or something *like* a hand!

The creature stood about as tall as Matthew, perhaps an inch or two taller, on goat legs but with a human-like upper body, though not altogether human. Its bare skin was reddish white, with splotchy hair about it, its face wide with a thick nose and very pronounced forehead with two horns growing out of it. Its hair was long and curly with a pointed beard on the chin. The hands, if you could call them that, were hoofy like a goat's or deer's yet with fingers. One of those hoofy hands was now held up in warning.

Matthew knew it immediately as a faun.

"Halt," said the faun. "In the name of the Alliance of Ainran, who seeks entry into the Garden?"

"Matthew Robinson, if you please, sir," replied Matthew.

"Let me introduce Rathnus," said Crynac coming up behind them. "He is one of the Guardians of the Gates. Rathnus, this is the boy of whom much has been spoken. He has come to the Forest at last. We of the King's Council have brought him to the Garden. In the name of the King, we request entrance."

The faun looked at Crynac, then walked closer and stared deeply and long into Matthew's eyes.

"Then pass, Wise one," he said at length. "And pass, son of Robin. Be welcome to the Garden of Ainran."

The faun stepped aside and stood solemnly at attention as the human and his five escorts walked past him and into the guardhouse.

Inside, set in an oak cabinet with a glass top, lay an enormous book, obviously very ancient. Its thick boards were lavishly decorated with pictures and old scripts. It was the kind of book a boy or girl might have looked at and thought boring, but which would make a grown-up tingle with excitement from its age.

"This is the Book," said Crynac. "It combines two volumes—the Book of the Prophecies and the Truths of Foundations. Its principles rule the Forest. In its early pages I discovered that concerning yourself which has led us to come here."

"But what is a faun doing here?" asked Matthew.

"The four entrances to the Garden are guarded by fauns sent from the land where the waters originate," replied Crynac. "There are many times that it takes failure to produce strength. Out of defeat and disappointment, the seeds are planted that grow courage, discernment, and wisdom. Such is the story of the permanent Commission of the Fauns. Their most famous ancestor slipped badly in his discernment where he lived on the borderlands of his kingdom. Out of his repentance for that failure, he grew strong, mighty, humble, and wise. Ever since his time, his descendents have been known for their keen intuition and discernment. For that reason they were appointed the border guardians of that land. Thus they were also chosen in the Alliance of Ainran to be sent to Pellanor to be the Guardians of the Gates. Though this is not their homeland, four fauns from Ainran are permanently stationed at the four guardhouses."

"Where are the others?" asked Matthew.

"You have been to the western gate," replied Crynac, "though we did not on that occasion pass through the gate itself. The Sword of Ainran sits not in the guardhouse but in front of the wall of rock through which entrance is gained. This is the Gate of the Book. East is the Gate of Fire, and north is the Gate of Blood. There may be time for you to examine the Book at more leisure another time. Now we must continue. The climax of our journey is at hand."

THIRTEEN

The Pool of Ainran

They left the guardhouse. They had only taken a few steps beyond it, a clear path now visible and beginning a descent, when Matthew stopped. His eyes shot open. The spectacle in front of him took his breath away.

Crynac the peregrine falcon, Ginger the prairie dog, Barnabas the fox, Chebab the monkey, and Shibnah the bear, to whom had been entrusted the safety of the Forest in the King's absence, all waited expectantly. They had been filled with hope as he led them past the crevice though the stone wall. But until the Garden and the Pool of Ainran blossomed fully before his eyes, Matthew would not be completely one of them. They glanced silently at one another and waited.

An audible gasp escaped Matthew's lips. At the sound, the five members of the Council knew that he *saw*. Obedience had been the opener of eyes.

"What do you see, Matthew?" asked Crynac.

"I see the most amazing beauty imaginable," replied Matthew slowly. "It is exactly as you told me it would be, yet infinitely more wondrous than words could describe—the circle of mountains on all sides, the green of lush fields and gardens and meadows extending in all directions, and the lake in front of us! I have never beheld such a sight!"

Spread out below, an emerald lake of unfathomable depth shimmered in the sunlight. Its surface was still, yet undulated slightly from the mighty waters surging up from deep within. Far in the distance, to his right, left, and straight ahead, Matthew saw three plumes of spray rising from the three falls flowing out into the three steep canyons leading north, east, and west. To his right and nearly straight down from their present vantage point, he heard the thunderous roar of the falls leading south, whose river they had been following for two days. From where they stood, almost straight below them, he could just make out one side of the falls where the deep translucent water poured out of the lake over a stone cliff edge and tumbled into the gorge below. From it, a great cloud of spray rose up to where they stood.

"Behold, Matthew," said Crynac, "the Pool of Ainran. Come, your destiny awaits."

They started down the path. The five led him through a fragrant pine wood. After a winding descent of another hour, at last they came to the water's edge. It was so beautiful and clear, and the air so still and warm, that Matthew wanted to change into his bathing suit and jump right in! But the other five were walking so slowly and solemnly, he could tell they felt great reverence for this place. It was no time to talk about having a swim!

Now for the first time Matthew saw what had not been visible from the overlook at the gatehouse. Across the green waters, a magnificent palace of white and gold rose against the trees and mountains. It seemed almost to emerge out of the water itself. Its heights reflected straight down into the fathomless depths of green.

"You are looking upon Sogol Pell Lealnor, home of the King," said Crynac.

They continued around the end of the lake and approached the castle. In awe Matthew gazed about him. As they drew closer, the higher and more ornate the palace appeared. Its turrets and towers stretched up into the blue of the sky itself.

Leading down from the massive oak doors of the entryway descended wide steps of purest white. Where they reached the level of the water, the expanse of marble continued, spreading out into a vast patio of white that stretched a great distance into the lake only an inch or two above the surface of the water.

Out onto this marble patio or pier, the five led Matthew until they were surrounded on three sides by water.

"Come, son of Robin," said Crynac, "be filled with healing, wholeness, and strength. For this you came. Now drink."

Matthew walked to the end of the marble platform, knelt on his hands and knees, bent his face to the water and set his lips to the green lake, and drank deeply.

It was like nothing he had ever tasted. With the first sip, he felt refreshing springs of living water surging into every part of him, all the way to his fingers and toes and the top of his head.

"You are drinking the Waters of Ainran, from which derives the life of all the Forest," said Crynac behind him. "Only the waters from this spring satisfy all thirsts, remove all cares, and bring peace in all things. They will give you strength, courage, and wisdom to face whatever unknowns the future holds. Henceforth, this is to be the divine well of your sustenance."

When Matthew stood a minute later, a new light shone from his eyes. The five knew that their mission had been rewarded. They saw the strength of a son of the King. They knew that he was ready to command them.

Matthew turned and walked back across the marble pier. The five members of the Forest Council knelt and bowed.

Matthew approached.

"Rise and stand tall before me," he said. "I am neither your King, nor yet your commander. Whatever else they may show me in time, the waters have revealed to me first and foremost my own weakness. I have seen that I know little and must learn much. The waters have shown me that the season is at hand for me to listen, to learn, and be trained in wisdom. That training must now begin. To you of the Council I entrust myself for it."

"It may well be," said Barnabas, "that such training is needed. But you are also our commander now, for such the King has decreed. What, then, would you have of us?"

Matthew drew a deep breath and thought a moment.

"Let us return to the Forest," he said. "As my first order of business, I want to know what can be done to rescue Spunky. If what you said before, Ginger, is true, that it was my fault, then I must see to his rescue. I must return to the Center of Enlightenment."

"You surely do not mean *yourself*?" said Ginger.

"Who else would I mean?"

"The danger is too great. For you to show yourself again at Argon's compound could prove fatal. We cannot risk your safety."

"What kind of leader would I be if I cannot do myself what I require others to do? I will listen to your counsel, but his rescue must ultimately fall to my hand. What about the other children of Pellanor? Are they also there?"

"We do not know for certain," replied Ginger. "Hopefully Spunky will have learned something. We fear that perhaps some have been sent off as servants to Dezreall's kingdom, even as—"

He hesitated, as if the thought was too hideous to say.

"—We fear some are being sold to the Kaldorites and Shelaharanites as domesticated *pets*."

A low growl sounded from Shibnah.

"Then that too must be among my first assignments. I must locate all the captives so that we will know what we are up against."

"What if the enemy again entices you with his elixir?" asked Chebab. "I do not mean to doubt you, Sire, but we are told to be wise as foxes and innocent as sheep."

"At last I know my own weakness for what it is," said Matthew. "I have not only seen the gate into the Garden. I have seen into myself. I am unworthy to be your leader. I agree to it only with your help. I know the elixir of *I-Am-Better* for the poison it is. I will not drink of it again."

Crynac smiled to himself. He Who Rules had chosen well. Humility was already growing within the boy. Because he did not think too highly of himself, wisdom would follow.

"Then let us repair to the Palace, and the King's armor room," said the falcon. "It is time you are outfitted with the weapons of Ainran that will protect you in battle and bring victory to our cause."

He led the way up the wide marble steps and to the great oak doors. They were not locked. Matthew followed the others inside. They walked up a wide circular marble staircase, up and around two more flights, and into a room paneled in rich dark wood. From the four walls hung weapons of every shape and kind—swords, shields, guns, muskets, coats of mail, helmets, and daggers.

Matthew looked around in wonder. Like all boys, he was fascinated with weapons. All at once he noticed that one of their number had disappeared.

"Where is Shibnah?" he asked.

The others turned behind them.

"I thought he was with us," said Ginger.

"Oh no!" exclaimed Barnabas. "You know what this means!"

He ran back out into the hall and along the corridor to a large window overlooking the lake.

"There he is!" cried Barnabas. "He is making for the cliff. Crynac, hurry—you've got to stop him!"

By now the others were clustered around the window. At first Matthew could not see what they were looking at. Then in the distance he saw Shibnah, who was so big he was hard to miss, scrambling up a steep series of boulders. At its top, a flat stone extended some distance straight out over the emerald waters.

"I fear it is too late, friend Barnabas," chuckled Crynac. "He has outwitted us again, the wise falcon and the clever fox."

Matthew saw Shibnah now reach the top. Without hesitation he lumbered toward the end of the flat protruding table of stone, and leapt with a mighty jump into the air. Matthew gasped at the sight, for by now he was easily a hundred feet above the water. With a gracefulness marvelous to behold, the huge bear slowly spun twice in the air, then plunged with his head straight below him deep into the icy depths of the pool. From the distance where they stood, it took a second for the sound of the splash to reach them. Suddenly a great watery *kaboom* exploded through the valley. When the echo off the mountains had faded away, all was silent again. Wavelets from the impact spread out in circles across the lake.

"I didn't know swimming was allowed," said Matthew. "I thought the waters were sacred."

"They are sacred waters indeed," said Crynac. "But there are no rules of holiness here, only the rule of kindness.

I have even seen the King swimming in the Pool of Ainran, for he is a King who loves to laugh. But the springs from beneath surge with mighty force. It is a wise animal, or human for that matter, who knows when to fear that power. Therefore, not many dare venture into these waters. But Shibnah is no ordinary bear. He is fearless. He loves nothing more than a good swim, the colder the water the better. Yet sometimes we fear he may be just a little to bold for his own good."

"Has something happened to him now?" asked Matthew with concern. "He hasn't come up yet."

"Be patient," said Chebab.

They watched the lake for what seemed an interminable time. After two or three minutes, far out in the middle suddenly the great brown form of Shibnah burst through the surface. He went on playing and cavorting, diving up and down for ten or fifteen minutes, to the great enjoyment of Matthew and the others.

When at last he swam to shore and leapt onto the white marble pier, the shaking of his great brown coat sent spray in every direction for twenty feet. Even after another great shimmying and jiggling of his enormous back and belly, his companions would not let him inside the Palace until they had gathered a dozen of the King's towels and, all five clustering about, they had thoroughly dried every inch of him.

FOURTEEN

Spunky's Troubles

You are probably wondering what happened to Spunky, and it is time we found out. About the same time that Matthew had suddenly turned grouchy after drinking Argon's elixir, you remember that Ginger had sent Spunky off to find Crynac the falcon so they could ask him what to do. Ginger planned to take Matthew to the Tall Tree and meet Spunky and Crynac there. But Matthew had stormed off and gone back to his grandparents', where he had also been grouchy to Timothy and Susanna.

Spunky went first to Crynac's underground den beneath the Tall Tree. But Crynac wasn't there. Chebab and the other guard-monkeys had no idea where he was. So Spunky left the Tall Tree in search of him.

Do you remember the crows that were hovering about watching Matthew after he left Argon's compound? From the air they were in contact with a small pack of fierce dogs on the ground. When Spunky began to cross an open meadow, the crows spotted him. Before he knew it, the dogs were after him. Spunky wasn't quick enough to get back to the trees. Suddenly he felt a dog's teeth grabbing him and picking him up by the scruff of the neck.

He thought he was dead right then, for there is nothing a mean dog likes for an afternoon snack as much as fresh prairie dog. But they were under orders to bring the prairie dogs back alive. So the dog ran back to Argon's palace with Spunky dangling from its mouth like a mother cat carrying a kitten, while the crows and other dogs continued their search. He didn't like it very much. But for once in his life Spunky managed to keep his mouth shut and say nothing. He knew he was lucky to be alive.

The dog took him straight to Argon and dumped Spunky on the floor at his feet. As soon as the dog was gone, Spunky found his voice. He had never seen Argon before, but he had heard enough about him that he knew exactly who he was.

"You'll never get away with this, you imposter!" he shouted. "You can't keep me here. You're no king. You're nothing but an old rattlesnake! I demand that you let me go."

If he had had a sword, he would have pulled it out and attacked Argon right there, even if he was only a fourth his height. Though he didn't fancy being eaten by a dog, Spunky wasn't frightened of anything.

"Tut, tut, Mr. Prairie Dog," said Argon calmly. "You mistake me. I admit that the method of your transport was perhaps a trifle unpleasant, but with their teeth is the only way dogs can carry things. They are such brutes, you know. I apologize for any discomfort you may have experienced. But I wanted to confer with you, and ask your advice on a matter of great importance. I know of the wisdom of the prairie dogs of the Forest. I have been told that the gray prairie dog called Spunky is the wisest of them all. I only wanted to ask if you knew this Spunky, and knew how I might contact him."

"Know him? Of course I know him," said Spunky. "I am Spunky Graytail."

"No! It cannot be! *You* are the famous Spunky of Pellanor?"

"I am."

"I cannot believe my good fortune! This is wonderful news! Then all the more I must apologize for your rough treatment by my dogs. I will speak to them and have them reprimanded. Would you like something to drink?"

Now Spunky was *very* hungry and thirsty by this time. But he had been well trained in the Truths of Foundations, and knew what he was about. He wasn't going to fall for a trick like that! He wasn't about to take so much as a sip of anything offered him in *this* place.

"No, thank you," he replied, deciding it would be best not to get angry again. He remembered the proverb out of the Book that you can catch more flies with honey than with vinegar. Until he managed to get out of there, it would probably be best to be cooperative.

"Very well," said Argon. "Perhaps later. I shall have my kitchen prepare something for you. You will be able to drink it at your leisure."

He turned and rang a little bell. A moment later the door opened and a bobcat walked in. A few hairs on the back of Spunky's neck stood on end. He felt a growl trying to rise in this throat—a prairie dog growl, of course. But he did not let it out. He did *not* like the look of the bobcat!

"Sheena," said Argon, "would you take our honored guest to the room prepared for him."

The bobcat led the way. With his skin crawling all over his body, Spunky followed. He glanced about as they went, trying to see what kind of place this was. The bobcat led him down a long flight of stairs into a basement, and to a bare room, where he left him. Spunky soon discovered just what Matthew had in the room they had taken him to, that the door was locked from the outside.

He sat down on the floor to think. It wasn't long before the door opened again. A girl walked in, a human Kaldorite by the look of it. She was carrying a tray. From it she removed a container, which she set down on the floor, then turned and left. She never once looked at Spunky or had any expression on her face. As she left, he thought he heard her saying softly in a sing-song voice, *I am happy here...I am always happy here...everyone is happy here.* The instant the door was closed behind her, the room filled with the tempting aroma of Argon's magic potion.

Of course the elixir that had been brought to Spunky's room wasn't the same as what Matthew had drunk. Whenever Argon was trying to get the Liberator inside someone new whom they had lured for a visit, he had a drink specially prepared exactly for them, with the perfect ingredients that would make them want to gulp it down. What he offered Spunky would not have appealed much to you or me—unless, that is, you happen to be a prairie dog or possibly a squirrel or a chipmunk. Nor was it in a silver goblet. It sat on the floor in a hollowed out gourd. It gave off smells of nuts and turnips and bulbs and certain very delicious roots and acorns and things like that.

To Spunky's nose it smelled like heaven.

It *had* been a long time since he had had anything to eat or drink. He was getting hungrier and thirstier by the minute.

FIFTEEN

Ancient Weapons

Meanwhile, at Sogol Pell Lealnor, Matthew and the five members of the King's Council had gathered again

"It is necessary, Matthew," said Crynac, "that the Council confer privately. Please wait for us here beside the waters. It will be a good time for you to reflect on what lies ahead. We will summon you shortly."

The five went inside and returned to the palace armory.

Perhaps twenty minutes later Chebab scampered up beside Matthew where he sat staring out over the restful expanse of emerald water.

"It is time," he said. "Please come."

Matthew followed him back into the Palace and up to where the others were gathered.

Cryac's wings were not very good at holding things, but with the help of the others, and with Shibnah reaching up on the wall for those mounted especially high, they had each selected a weapon to be taken down and given to Matthew to prepare him for the battles ahead.

"All the weapons you see in this room are the King's personal property," said Crynac. "You will notice that they are not new. They show signs of battles fought and battles won, by our own King and his predecessors, going all the way back in some cases to Maharba the Great himself. Before he went away, the King left to our discretion which would be most needful in our present crisis, and which would be most suited to your personal strengths and weaknesses."

"First," said Crynac, "I have chosen for you the King's Shield of Innocence. It will enclose your character with the grace of childlikeness from the Garden, and protect you from the lethal darts of the Liberator. You will see that the tip of the top right corner is missing. It was sliced off during battle in ancient times, reminding us of the dangers the innocent will always face in life. But its strength also saved the life of the King who wielded it, as it will all who carry it."

"These Boots of Truthfulness," said Chebab, setting two well worn leather boots on the floor in front of him, "will guide your way no matter how dark the path."

Shibnah now held out a sword in a bright gold sheath. It was not huge. The silver blade measured some three feet in length, just the right size for a boy of Matthew's build which he could wield comfortably. Shibnah extended his two great paws toward Matthew with the sword laying across them.

"Shibnah bestows upon you the Sword of Justice," said Ginger. "Its hilt is of pure white gold, mined from deep within the slopes of Mount Kindness and wrapped with the fine unbreakable hair from the tail of a unicorn of Ainran. It was the unicorn's dying wish that the hair from his tail, along with his horn, containing mighty magical powers, be given as a gift to our King. The three knobs you see on the sword's handle were fashioned from that horn. Together, the blade and hilt will enable you to wage war against deception without anger, prejudice, vengeance, and with a heart of love, whatever evils may have to be slain with it. Many peculiar tales are told of the exploits of this sword, which can be explained in no other way than that it possesses unknown powers in the great battle for eternal Justice."

Shibnah nodded to him. Matthew took hold of the sword, then strapped it around his waist with the leather belt attached to the sheath.

"Having known you longer than any of the others," now said Ginger, "I have chosen for you the Helmet of Purity. Like the shield of childlikeness, it will protect you from sinking to the level of those around you. Let no word of unkindness, no oath, no loose talk, no gossip, no ridicule, no unkind or ungracious speech, no criticism nor rebuke pass your lips. You are the King's son, a prince of the Forest. You must walk with dignity befitting that calling."

"For my choice," said Barnabas, "I have selected from among the King's possessions one that many would not consider a weapon at all. But in the battle against the Liberator it may perhaps be the most important of all. It is the Cloak of Humility. It was made for the great-grandfather of the present King before his famous battle at Mons Eagleglen against the Kaldorites. The leather is from the hide of the great buffalo Thunderhoof who was the first to fall in that battle. Before leading the charge, should he not survive, he asked that the King would use his skin to make for himself a protective coat. If you others would join me," he said turning to his companions, "let us come together to lay over Matthew's shoulders the legendary tunic of King Josiah of the Glen."

The others drew close. All five, though Crynac struggled a bit to grasp it, took hold of a portion of the tunic Barnabas had removed from the wall. Matthew knelt on one knee as they gently hung it over his shoulders. Matthew rose and laced up its leather straps. His fingers were better suited for that kind of thing than paws.

"All these weapons will be invisible to those on the outside," said Crynac. "They can only be seen by those with the eyes of the Forest."

"Will they make me invisible?" asked Matthew.

"No. You will only appear to their eyes as an ordinary boy. They will see nothing that has its origins in the Garden. As you wear and wield these weapons," the falcon added, "remember that the magic of the Garden is infused with the air of selflessness. It is selflessness that enables you to see, and selfishness that prevents the enemy's people from true vision. Therefore, do nothing merely to please yourself. Always think of the effect of your actions and words on others. Such is the way of our Kings and their princes.

"And finally," said Crynac, "you will take with you the magic flask of Maharba the Great. — Barnabas, please."

The fox walked across the armory, opened a small case in which were stored many smaller items, and removed from it a silver flask covered with white leather upon which was embossed in red the coat of arms of the Kings of the Forest. He brought it back and handed it to Matthew.

"This is one of the oldest items in the palace," said Crynac. "It was forged by the dwarfs of Alnath as a gift to the King and has been in the possession of his descendents ever since. It is a magic flask. When filled from the waters of Ainran, it will never run dry so long as it is used to carry out the Will of the King. Once you fill it with the sacred waters, use it wisely and well."

Crynac paused, then added solemnly,

"Now go, Matthew, son of Robin and son of the King. We five charge you to faithfully step into the destiny prepared for you from before time began."

SIXTEEN

The New Commander's First Decision

The six spent the night in the Palace fortifying themselves for what lay ahead with food and drink from the Garden. They set out on their return journey bright and early the next morning. They reached Miss Fernduddle's by midday. All morning Matthew had been revolving an idea in his mind. Now he told the others what he wanted to do.

"I have decided, as I said before, to return to Argon's compound," he said. "And alone. I need only for one or all of you to guide me far enough that I can find the rest of the way on my own. Then you must return and spread through the Forest to rally our support and encourage the families with hope. Discouragement is our great enemy. You must tell them not to give up, that the rescue of their children will soon begin. I will try to find Spunky, and learn what I can about the others."

Matthew knew they would probably object. And they did. He was surprised, however, when Crynac consented to his plan, with the proviso that Silverwing and his squadron of sparrows be allowed to patrol the skies above him until he reached the border.

Later that day they parted. By the next afternoon, Matthew was alone in the Forest, moving southwest.

He was feeling lonely but strangely invigorated for what lay ahead. He had begun to realize what a great responsibility rested on his shoulders.

He wasn't sure what he was going to do for the night. He still had plenty of Miss Fernduddle's provisions. But he wasn't used to sleeping in the woods alone. He was, we must remember, only fourteen, though he was growing older by the minute.

Just as it was getting dark, suddenly a great flurry around his head made him look up. There was Silverwing the Sparrow circling down toward him with a dozen of his friends.

"I trust all is well, Sire," he said.

"No sign of trouble down here," said Matthew. "How does it look from the sky?"

"So far so good. We will hope the morrow proves as uneventful. By then, however, the enemy's crows will have seen that Beathnah's patrol has suddenly retreated north. It may make them curious to widen their flights. Still, I think we can manage to keep you out of their sight. Where were you planning to spend the night?"

"I was just wondering that," said Matthew.

"With your permission," said Silverwing, "might I suggest the treetops. There is an abandoned eagle's aerie not far from here. We could guide you to it. I think you would find it most comfortable."

"I, uh...is it terribly high in the trees?" asked Matthew.

"Oh yes, at the very top."

"You do remember that I am not a bird? How will I get to it?"

"I am confident the tree is one you will be able to climb."

"I will try. But if I get scared of falling, I may have to find someplace on the ground."

Within an hour, Matthew was climbing up the tree where Silverwing's squadron had led him. He had needed some help getting up to the first branch, which was a good way above his head. But with a few strong vines stretched over it by Silverwing's birds, he managed to pull himself up the trunk, then hoist a leg over the branch. From there it was a smooth climb all the way until the trunk narrowed and began to sway a bit. Then it became a little fearsome. Matthew paused and took a sip from the King's flask. After that he felt his courage renewed and he scrambled the rest of the way without looking down once.

When he crept into the eagle's nest he found it big enough for several humans. He could have a sleepover with friends in a nest *this* big! He had forgotten that eagles in this Forest were probably bigger than him!

He made himself a nice supper of cheese, biscuits of oat with smoked fish, and of course water from the flask, and was soon fast asleep.

It took Matthew two more days, moving slowly, to reach the border southwest of the Forest. The next night he slept in a rabbit warren Silverwing had arranged to borrow for the night. It wasn't as comfortable as the eagle's nest, and a little prickly. But it was safe from prying crows' eyes and that was the most important thing. His last night in the Forest he was finally treated to a night in a beaver's lodge, which was something he had always wanted to do. It had been built in a stream that forked east from the Calumia. After riding across their pond on the back of Widetail, his beaver hosts made him feel like one of the family—at least as much as beavers could for a boy!

On the third day, in the middle of the afternoon, Silverwing flew down to him again.

"This is where we must leave you, Sire," he said. "The border is ahead about half a mile. We must not fly closer or our presence might alert them to your presence."

"Thank you very much, Silverwing."

"Be careful, Sire, and good luck."

"Thank you. And believe me, I will be careful!"

SEVENTEEN

Outside the Compound

From where Matthew lay on his belly looking out from amongst the trees, the whole of Argon's compound spread out before him. Not so much activity surrounded the place as before. The sheep and cows grazing a couple fields over looked like ordinary sheep and cows. That was probably as good a place to try to make an entry as anywhere, Matthew thought. He could hardly imagine a *mean* cow or sheep!

Carefully he crept out of the cover of the trees and toward them, inching and slinking along in the tall grass. He managed to squeeze under the wire of a fence. After ten or fifteen minutes he had crawled into the same field where the sheep and cows were munching away.

When he was as close as he dared get, he stopped and sat up. He was still a good distance from the animals. As he sat in the field he intentionally pretended not to notice them. Everyone knows that if you approach animals too quickly, it frightens them and they run off. But if you are patient and let an animal's natural curiosity work on them, before long they might approach.

So Matthew waited, pretending to take no notice. Perhaps ten minutes later he heard the soft sound of footsteps (or *hoof* steps!) in the grass behind him.

"Excuse me, young man," said a soft, woolly, melodic voice. "Aren't you one of the young princes?"

Matthew turned to see a large sheep approaching with a look of question on its face.

"Hello," he said. "Yes, I am Prince Matthew."

He had hoped that perhaps out in the fields the animals might not have heard about his leaving and escaping back to the Forest.

"I have not seen you again since the day we celebrated your arrival," said the sheep.

"I have been very busy," said Matthew. "But you all seem so peaceful out here, I thought there must be something special about your field."

"Oh, there is! The grass is far better than where we came from. We are happy here. We are all very happy. But—" he added, then hesitated a moment. "Do you mind if I ask you a question—what is it like in the palace? Is it very fine indeed?"

"I would say so," replied Matthew. "Have you never been inside?"

"Sheep and cattle are not allowed inside. King Argon says that is only for those worthy to be called his own children. We are not allowed to call him Father Argon like the others, you see. He says we are not smart enough to understand the secrets his children know about. I know I am not very smart, but I would like to learn some of the secrets. We are all his children, but some are more his children than others. They are his special children. Still, I am happy here, because we are all very happy here."

"Are prairie dogs allowed to call him Father?" asked Matthew. "Are *they* allowed inside the palace to learn the secrets?"

"I don't know," replied the sheep. "I did think I saw a prairie dog a few days ago. Now that you mention it, they were taking him to the house. I don't know if he was a new visitor. There was no feast in his honor. A big doberman was carrying him inside. I thought that the poor prairie dog must have hurt his leg and couldn't walk."

"Have you seen him since?" asked Matthew. "I would like to see him. I am curious whether prairie dogs are told the secrets. I am still new, you see. I am trying to understand everything myself."

"I thought you human princes knew *everything*."

"Oh no. That's why I would like to talk to the prairie dog, just like I am talking to you. I wonder where I could find him. I don't want to bother Argon."

"Don't you mean *Father* Argon? Surely that's what *you* call him."

"Yes, of course. But he is so busy, you know."

"Why don't you ask Sheena," said the sheep. "She knows *almost* everything. Or Queen Dezreall?"

"Perhaps I shall. But do *you* have any idea where I might find the prairie dog?"

"Sometimes they take the wounded animals, the ones the dogs bring in, to the basement. That is where the Rooms of Healing and Reeducation are. That's what they are called, though I am not sure what that means. I have never seen them. But that is where the wounded recover. They always come out happy because everyone is happy after they have been healed. They are given special medicines and drinks so that they will get better and be very happy here."

Again, a puzzled expression came over the sheep's face.

"If you don't mind my asking, young Prince," he said slowly, "what is that peculiar thing you are wearing over half of your shoulder?"

"What peculiar thing?" asked Matthew.

"I cannot tell what it is. It looks like very old leather, but…oh, I must have been mistaken. It is gone now. My eyes were playing tricks on me. I am not very smart, you understand. But I am very happy here."

Matthew was suddenly very interested in this sheep! He had seen part of his tunic! He had not completely lost his Forest eyesight!

"What is your name?" Matthew asked.

"My name is Baalemel. Everyone just calls me Lemmie."

"Well, Mr. Baalemel," said Matthew, "perhaps you can help me. I would like to find a way into the Rooms of Healing from outside the palace. Do you think that is possible?"

"But why?"

"I cannot tell you. It would have to be a secret, just between us. You said you wanted to know some of the palace secrets. This concerns the greatest secret of all. I promise to tell you all about it some day very soon—even things that those who live inside the palace do not know. Do you think you might trust me."

"I don't know. It is a strange request, but I might *try* to trust you."

"That is all I can ask of you."

The sheep called Baalemel thought a moment. "I might have a word with Earthshover the groundhog. He knows everything about the underground regions. He is much cleverer than me."

"Do you think I would fit into any of his tunnels?"

"He is a very fat groundhog. If there was a way into the palace through his tunnels, he would know about it."

"But it will be our secret," said Matthew.

"I will try to remember. But I will have to wait for Earthshover to come up for a bit of fresh air. I cannot go to *him*."

"I understand, Mr. Baalemel," said Matthew. "I will wait for you here. Tell me, before you go, are you thirsty?"

"A little, I think."

"Would you like a drink, if you can drink from my hand? I have the best water you have ever tasted."

Matthew took out the King's flask and poured out a little water with one hand as he cupped his other to hold it. The sheep took a few steps forward, then lapped at it with his tongue.

"That is delicious water indeed," he said. "Perhaps…might I have just a little more?"

"Of course," said Matthew. He poured more into his hand, and then a third time.

"Oh, there it is again!" exclaimed the sheep as it lifted its head and stared at Matthew's shirt. "Only now the strange thing hanging from your shoulder is larger. It is spreading halfway across your chest!"

"It is part of the secret I will tell you about later," said Matthew. "I think I can safely promise that you will soon know all about it—though it may surprise you!"

"I like surprises!"

When Baalemel left him to go in search of Earthshover, Matthew saw him skipping into the air a time or two bounding energetically across the field.

EIGHTEEN

In the Dungeon of Healing

When Spunky heard a key in the lock of the door to his room and the latch from outside turn, he expected to see one of the girls or animals who came bringing him nuts and beets and carrots. They were the driest nuts he had ever eaten in his life, and the beets and carrots were too shriveled to eat. Without something to wash them down, he could hardly eat anything. No water had yet come with them. He knew what they wanted him to drink!

He glanced up and saw the last person he expected to see walking into his room.

"Matthew!" exclaimed Spunky.

"Hello, Spunky," said Matthew, glancing about. "So these are the Rooms of Healing!"

"Healing my paw! A dungeon is more like it—I'm locked in! How did you get in?"

"Never mind that right now. Let's just say I have made acquaintance with one of your distant relatives—a groundhog by the name of Earthshover, who is, I might add, not particularly delicate about whose face he shoves dirt in! Once I was inside the basement, the rest was easy. The key is hanging outside on the wall."

"What are you doing here?" said Spunky. "Are you one of them now?"

"Of course not. Do you think this dirt is all over me because I am an honored guest?"

"You expect me to believe you? The last time I saw you, you called the Wise One a stupid old falcon. You had drunk the enemy's poison and it was obvious it had done its work. If you want to know the truth—you were a miserable brute of a boy."

"You're right, I was," said Matthew. "But much has happened since then, Spunky. You have to believe me—I am on your side now. I've come to rescue you."

"Why should I believe you? How could you have got in here unless you're one of them?"

"If I was one of them, I wouldn't have had to crawl in through a groundhog's tunnel! Tell me, Spunky," said Matthew, "what do you see? What am I wearing?"

"Come to think of it—you do look different," said Spunky. "You're wearing a leather tunic, boots that look like nothing you were wearing before, with leather sides and straps to the knees. And now that I look more carefully, you have a sword hanging from your belt! There is something different in your eyes, too."

"At least your sight is still good," said Matthew. "You must not have drunk the poison," said Matthew. "By the way," he added, glancing around the room, "what is that horrid smell!"

"Isn't it heavenly!"

"It's ghastly!"

"I think it is the most wonderful thing I have ever smelled in my life," said Spunky, pointing across the floor. "Look, it's over there, in that gourd. It's the elixir."

"It doesn't smell like what he gave me!"

"They brought it to me three days ago. It has been intoxicating my brain ever since. It's all I can do to keep away from it. But I daren't drink. I am weak from thirst. I've hardly had a thing to eat either."

"Then have a drink of this," said Matthew, pulling the flask from inside his tunic.

"Why should I drink what you give me," said Spunky, growing suspicious again. "This could be a trick. It might be more of the same potion!"

"Smell it, Spunky," said Matthew. He removed the lid and cork and held it toward Spunky's nose. "What do you smell?"

Skeptically Spunky sniffed once or twice. "I have to admit," he said, "it doesn't smell anything like what they brought me. It makes me think of blue skies, high mountains with snow on them, white marble towers glistening with the gold of the sun, and—"

Suddenly Spunky paused, a look of wonder on his face. "Where did this water come from?" he asked.

"Look, Spunky," said Matthew. "Peer into the flask. What do you see?"

Spunky bent his face over the open flask.

"I see the deep green of purest emerald," he said reverently.

"This flask was filled from the Pool of Ainran," said Matthew.

"You were at the Pool of Ainran!"

"I was," nodded Matthew. "Accompanied by Ginger and the rest of the King's Council. Everything I am wearing came from the armory at Sogol Pell Lealnor."

"You have been inside the King's Palace!" Spunky exclaimed.

"I hope that will tell you whose side I am on now. This is the flask of Maharba the Great."

Spunky hesitated no longer. He grabbed the flask from Matthew's hand, clutched it between his paws, threw his head back, and drank and drank.

When at last his thirst was quenched, he removed the flask from his lips and handed it again to Matthew.

"I'm sorry," he said. "I seem to have drunk it all. I hope you're not thirsty at the minute."

"Not to worry," smiled Matthew. "Look."

Again he held the flask and Spunky peered inside. To his surprise saw that the flask was still full.

"As long as we obey the Truths of Foundations," Matthew said, "this flask will be continually renewed with the Waters of Ainran."

"Well, I feel a new prairie dog!" said Spunky, his legs and paws tingling and itching for battle. "Let's bust out of here and give that Argon a bit of his own back! You don't happen to have an extra sword on you?"

"Not so fast, Spunky," said Matthew. "You and I cannot fight the deception alone. We have to find where they are keeping the other children, and make sure no one finds out we are here. It's about winning the war, Spunky, not a single battle."

"I would still like to challenge that pretender to a duel."

"Plenty of time for that later. Do you know if all the captive children are here? There is a rumor that some of them have been moved elsewhere."

"It's true," said Spunky. "Most are here, but some are in Kaldorah. Another thing I got wind of," he added. "There is a plot to assassinate the King."

"Argon!"

"No—he's no king! I mean our own King, He Who Rules, the rightful King of Pellanor."

"Do you know any details?"

"Only that Argon and Dezreall's son Ian has been sent after the King to make sure he does not return home. He has been given special power by the Liberator to hide his true motives."

"That is their specialty all right! Duplicity is their M.O."

Matthew thought a moment.

"Spunky," he said, "you must sneak back to the Forest to warn the Council. They must get word to the King."

"What about you?" asked Spunky. "Why don't we bust out of here together?"

"I've got to remain here for a while," replied Matthew. "I have discovered that the magic elixir does not necessarily destroy Forest eyesight completely. There may be some who are ready to return to their families. If there is any chance of getting even a single one out, I have to try. The first few that are set free are the most important. After that, their hold on the children will begin to weaken. But we cannot delay warning Crynac."

"How will I get out without them spotting me?"

"The same way I got in. I'll take you to the tunnel. The only dangerous part will be after you reach the open field. Once you get to the trees, no crow or dog is going to bother you."

"What should I do then?"

"Find Ginger. You two weren't named watchmen of the Forest for nothing. Get to Crynac and tell him what you heard."

Two minutes later, Matthew cautiously opened the door, then led Spunky out into the deserted basement to the opening into Earthshover's domain.

"The tunnel is pitch black," he said. "Keep going until you see daylight. If you run into the groundhog, you'll have to think of something to tell him. Once you are in the open air you will be in a field full of grazing cattle and sheep. Act confident and ask for a sheep called Lemmie."

"Lemmie! Who's that?"

"One of the sheep. I'm pretty sure we can trust him. Tell him that you are the prairie dog the prince was looking for and that you have been sent on a special mission by the prince. Tell him I asked him to help you by shielding you from sight from the house. Tell him to walk along with you as you make your way to the edge of the field. He will ask why. He is full of questions. Tell him that you are on a secret mission for the prince and no one must know about it. Tell him the prince promises to tell him all about it very soon. Get to the Tall Tree and tell Crynac what you have learned. I will meet you at the Tall Tree tomorrow, or the next day at the latest. Wait for me there. — Now go, Spunky!"

NINETEEN

Spunky's Escape

A s soon as Spunky was gone, Matthew hurried back into the room where they had kept him. He had spoken bravely and confidently about staying behind. But he didn't really know how he was going to find out if any children were ready to go home.

But Matthew was learning something about what happens when one drinks water from the Pool of Ainran, if one's heart is as pure as the high emerald waters. He was finding out that if you are faithful to take the one next step that is shown you, another will be shown you to follow, and another after that. Before you know it, you are walking along a path out of your perplexity that you couldn't see before.

Matthew had known that it was important to get Spunky on his way to warn the King. That had been his first step. Then he had to be patient for the next thing he was supposed to do to reveal itself.

Before that, however, Spunky was well on his way to the Tall Tree. He had a much better time of it in the groundhog's tunnel than Matthew did. He was used to that sort of thing. An underground tunnel was as easy for him as walking in bright sunlight. He came to many forks. Whenever he took one that gradually seemed to go back in the direction of the house, he turned around and tried another. And of course he had Matthew's scent to guide him. Eventually he began to see a little light ahead. It grew brighter. At last the tunnel bent steeply up and out into the air.

Spunky poked his head very slowly into the sunshine, squinted, and glanced around. There was the house behind him. He hadn't come as far as the field with the sheep and cattle. He was still too close to the stables and paddocks. He must have taken a wrong turn somewhere. He wasn't about to go back now. For in the distance he saw the trees of the Forest! It was all he could do not to make a dash for it right then. But he knew he needed to obey what Matthew had said. He was the King's commander now.

He crept out of the tunnel and slowly inched his way toward the sheep. He was too close to the house for comfort. He didn't dare break into a run for fear of attracting attention.

After what seemed forever, he scrunched low beneath the fence, then stood up on his four short legs and walked toward the sheep nearest him. He remembered what Matthew had told him about acting confident.

"Mr. Sheep," he said, "I've been sent to find someone called Lemmie."

The sheep picked up its head, a few blades of grass hanging from its mouth, and looked at Spunky. If he was surprised to see a prairie dog half his size in his field, he didn't show it.

"He's over there," he replied, dropping some of the grass as he spoke. "He's with that group of three. Lemmie's the one with the long tail."

Spunky thanked him and walked toward the three sheep, trying not to hurry so nobody would think he was up to anything suspicious.

"Hello," he said as he approached, "are you the one they call Lemmie?"

One of the three sheep lifted its head and looked at him. "That's me," he said.

"Might I have a word with you in private?" said Spunky. "It is a very important matter. I am here on the King's business."

Now the other two sheep glanced up. The surprised looks on their faces showed that they were impressed that Lemmie was so important!

Spunky motioned with his head and began walking away. Lemmie slowly followed. When they were far enough away that they wouldn't be heard, Spunky stopped.

"The prince sent me to find you, Lemmie," he said. "I am the prairie dog he was looking for. The prince needs your help again on very important business."

"The prince needs *my* help?" said Lemmie. "Why does he want my help?"

"He asked you to help me. I am on a secret mission. He said that only you could help me."

"Did he tell you that I am not very smart?"

"No, he said you were a very clever sheep, and that you would help me. He wanted me to tell you that he would explain everything to you very soon. Can you help me?"

"I can try."

"Then I need you to shield me from view so that I can walk over there toward the Forest. No one must know. The prince wants you to walk along with me and let me hide under your wool coat as I walk along through the grass until we get close to the Forest."

"That doesn't sound very hard. Perhaps I can do that."

"Then let's go. I am in a big hurry to be off on the prince's business. — Come, Lemmie."

Still a little confused, Lemmie began to walk. Spunky crouched beneath him and slowly they moved off from the other sheep toward the edge of the field closest to the border of the Forest. Their progress was slow, because Lemmie was confused about who was supposed to lead and who was supposed to follow. He kept stopping and waiting. Spunky had to keep telling him to walk toward the Forest and that he would walk along beneath him.

Gradually they moved closer and closer toward the edge of the field.

But all Argon's most *special* children, though it was never said in so many words, were also trained as guards. They kept on the lookout for anyone behaving oddly. Though they were all very happy there, Argon and Dezreall did not like *too* much individuality. That might mean someone was thinking for himself. They said it was dangerous to think for oneself. So when anyone acted like they were getting too independent, they were watched very carefully.

Spunky and Lemmie were just about to the edge of the field when a little girl racoon, who happened to be Gideon Racoon's daughter though she now called Dezreall her mother, saw a sheep in the field walking in a most peculiar manner away from the rest of the sheep. If she didn't know better she would think it was drunk! She went immediately to tell Sheena the bobcat. Sheena summoned one of the fastest dogs to investigate.

A few seconds later, Spunky heard the fierce barking of a huge Doberman Pincer coming their way...and fast! By now were close enough to the tall grass of the next field that he thought he might be able to keep from being seen.

"Thank you, Lemmie!" he said. "It's time I said good bye!"

Spunky shot out from between Lemmie's front legs and made a dash for the fence. Seconds later he was squirming under the wire and sprinting for the Forest. When he had gone what he thought was far enough, he stopped and crouched flat on his belly in the tall grass. He hoped he was invisible to the charging Doberman. Carefully he turned around to look.

The dog was barking ferociously and came running straight at Lemmie, who had turned around to face him. Just as he reached him, Lemmie lowered his head as if he had been a goat and butted the dog straight in the face. Stunned and surprised, the great Doberman sprawled out over the grass, not quite sure what had happened. He came to his senses soon enough. He jumped up with a mean growl in his throat.

"You will pay for that, you stupid sheep!" he shouted.

He opened his mouth showing two rows of sharp teeth, sprang toward Lemmie, and champed down on one of his legs. Poor Lemmie baa-ed in pain and fell over, blood pouring from the wound. Still growling, the Doberman began to back up with Lemmie's leg crushed between its jaws, and dragged him toward the house.

Spunky growled quietly. The legs of his muscles twitched to run out and join the fight. But he knew how foolish that would be. He remembered what Matthew had said about winning the war not the battle. All he could do was watch in horror. As soon as the Doberman was out of sight and close to the house, Spunky stood and dashed through the grass to the trees. Five minutes later he was surrounded by the safety of the Forest and scampering among the shadows northward toward the Tall Tree.

TWENTY

The Tide Begins to Turn

Back in the basement of the so-called palace, Matthew was still waiting to be shown what to do next. He had put the key of the lock back on the hook where it was kept outside the door. He wedged a tiny sliver of wood into the lock so the door would close without locking him inside.

About three hours later he heard footsteps coming in the hallway outside. Four feet sounded on the floor instead of two, so he knew it was an animal not a human—and a hoofed animal rather than one with pads on its feet. He stood and put his foot to the door and leaned his body against it so that whoever it was wouldn't be able to open it.

"Please don't come in just now," he said, doing his best to imitate Spunky's voice. "I am very tired."

"Wouldn't you like something to eat?" said an animal sounding voice. "I have some nice nuts for you."

"I am not hungry," said Matthew.

"Perhaps then you should have something to drink," she said. She had been told to remind Spunky about the elixir. If he got thirsty enough, they knew he would have to drink it eventually.

"That is a good idea," Matthew replied. "In fact I think I will. I will have a drink right now."

He took out the flask from the pocket of his tunic and took a nice long drink.

"That was the most delicious thing I have ever tasted in my life," he said. "Do you mind if I ask you a question?"

"I suppose not," answered whoever it was from outside the door.

"Are you really happy here?" asked Matthew.

There was a long hesitation.

"I don't know," said the voice slowly. "I must be, mustn't I? They tell us we are happy here, that we must be happy here because our parents no longer control us."

"But are you really happy here? Do you ever miss your parents?"

Another long silence followed. On a hunch, though it could have been a dangerous thing to do, Matthew removed his foot from the bottom of the door and stepped back.

He waited several more seconds. Slowly the door opened a crack, then all the way. There stood a young deer with a forlorn expression in her big round eyes. Matthew saw that she was on the verge of tears.

"I do miss my mummy," she said. Slowly she began to cry.

All of a sudden she realized she was looking at a human boy.

"You aren't the prairie dog," she said.

"I am Prince Matthew," said Matthew. "Surely you remember me."

"What are you doing in the Rooms of Healing."

"I was sent to you."

"Me?"

"I am here on the King's business."

"But what is that you are wearing? And why do you have a sword hanging from your belt?"

In that instant Matthew knew what his next step was—to get this innocent young doe back to her family!

"Where is the prairie dog?" the girl asked.

"He has gone back to the Forest," replied Matthew.

"I sometimes wish I could go back."

"Do you really want to?"

"Yes, but they won't let me. They tell me that this is my home now. Dezreall keeps telling me that she is my mummy. But I want my real mummy and daddy."

"I could take you back to them."

"Could you? Could you really?"

"Yes, if you want to go. It would be dangerous. You would have to be very brave."

"I don't know if I can be as brave as a prince."

"You only have to be as brave as you are required to be. Are there others like you who want to go back to the Forest?"

"I don't know. They all say they are happy here."

"Then you and I will return to the Forest alone. Can you trust me and do whatever I tell you?"

"I will try."

"Are you ready to go *today*?"

"Oh, yes! Do you mean it? Will you really take me back to the Forest where I will never have to see Dezreall and Sheena again?"

"By tonight you will be safely in the Forest. Only you must do exactly as I say."

"Oh, I will, I promise!"

"Then have a drink of this water," said Matthew, pouring a little from the flask into one of his hands. "It will help you be brave." The young doe lapped it up.

"Where did you get that!" she exclaimed. "That tastes like water from the Forest near where I live. It reminds me of home."

"It is from the Forest," said Matthew. "What is your name?"

"I am Raennel. May I have just a little more?"

"You may have as much as you like," said Matthew. He held the flask to her lips and tipped it so that she could drink freely. He could already see life coming back into her eyes.

"Now, Raennel," said Matthew. "I want you to go back upstairs and continue with your normal activities for the rest of the day. Keep your head down. If anyone looks you in the eye they will immediately see the light in your eyes from drinking the water of the Forest. Pretend that everything is the same. When can you get outside without being noticed?"

"After supper I have to go outside for the night. I am not allowed to sleep in the house."

"Then we will go after supper. Can you get to the field where the cattle and sheep graze?"

"Oh, can I! I can jump all the fences. The only reason I don't run away is the dogs. I am terribly frightened of the dogs. They can run as fast as I can. They are very mean."

"You leave the dogs to me. I will be hiding in the field with the sheep. If you can be brave enough to make a dash for that field, the dogs will not harm you. There is a sheep who will help us named Lemmie."

"He is not in the field anymore," said Raennel. "He has a broken leg. He was dragged in by one of Sheena's Dobermans for being a bad sheep. I think he will be down in the rooms of healing before long."

"I see. Well, I will be in the field waiting for you. Now go. Remember, pretend that everything is normal until after supper."

The rest of the day passed slowly for Matthew. After another hour or two he heard a commotion outside. He heard the snarling of dogs and a *bump, bump, bumping* like they were dragging something down the stairs, with moaning sheep sounds along with it. He suspected it was poor Lemmie. He heard a door clank shut and the dogs returned upstairs.

Slowly he crept out of his room, listened at the other doors until he heard soft crying from behind one of them. Quickly he located the key and let himself in. There lay Lemmie on the floor, his beautiful white wool coat matted and smeared with the red of his own blood.

"Oh, Prince," said Lemmie feebly. "I am sorry, I do not think I was much help."

"Lemmie, of course you were," said Matthew. "What happened?"

"The prairie dog got away on his secret mission. I had to stop Rauchmull from chasing him. But I made him angry, so he bit me and broke my leg."

"You have the courage of a lion, Lemmie!" said Matthew. "I am very proud of you. I promise that the King himself will hear of your bravery. Now take a long drink of this.

Again Matthew took out his flask, opened Lemmie's mouth and tipped it back so that he could pour the healing water straight into his mouth. After he had had a long drink, he also poured it liberally all over the wound on his leg.

"I must leave you, Lemmie," said Matthew. "Continue to be brave. I am sure you will feel better before long. I will come back for you soon."

Matthew left him. It was now time for him to go. He found his way back to Earthshover's tunnel. He was not looking forward to trying to find his way back outside underground, but he had no choice. Into the tunnel he ducked, crawling on his hands and knees as far as he could go. Then he had to inch along the rest of the way flat on his belly. He was glad he hadn't brought the great shield from the King's armory! He would never have been able to wriggle through the little tunnel with *that*!

It took him a long time to reach the field. Eventually, face and hair and sword hilt and tunic all covered with dirt, he again felt the fresh air on his face. He looked about to get his bearings. He decided that it would be best to stay hidden in the tunnel. He didn't want to risk being seen before Raennel made her dash away from the house.

The late afternoon wore on slowly. Just as dusk was beginning to set in, suddenly he heard shouts.

"After her!" barked a dog's voice. "The fool deer is running for the fields! Get her! Don't let her reach the trees!"

Matthew was out of the tunnel in an instant. Raennel was bounding over the fence by the stables. She bounced across the yard and leapt the next fence in a great spring. Matthew sprinted for the field of sheep and quickly climbed the fence.

Raennel flew toward him over the grass like the wind. Three Dobermans were after her and moving just as fast. She saw Matthew and made straight for him. He saw terror but also exhilaration in her eyes.

She flew into the air and leapt several feet high over Matthew's head.

"Keep on!" he shouted as she soared over his head. "Make for the Forest! I will be right behind you!"

Within seconds she had reached the fence on the opposite side of the field.

Matthew did not see her leap it, for he now turned to face her pursuers. The dogs came on, teeth gleaming and dripping with evil purpose. Matthew stood tall, yanked out the Sword of Justice from its sheath and pointed it toward them.

The lead Doberman slowed, its lips twitching, its fangs hungry for blood. Seeing nothing of Matthew's tunic or sword, he was not frightened in the least. All he saw was a little kid with his arm in the air.

"Do you think you can stop us, boy?" he snarled. "Get away and we will let you live. The deer-child is no concern of yours. She belongs to us. Now stand aside or die with her!"

"You are a coward, you low cur!" shouted Matthew, not budging an inch. "To go after an innocent doe with the heart of a child is evil. You may take my life, but you will not touch her!"

With a movement so sudden his legs were a blur, the wrathful Doberman let out a roar of fury and sprang forward, jaws wide and aimed at Matthew's throat.

Matthew raised the sword, ducked suddenly to his left, and with mighty force thrust the blade deep into the dog's chest five inches below the neck. Blood spewed as the huge beast fell with a great thud, dead at his feet. Matthew withdrew the sword and ran toward the other two.

"In the name of the King of the Forest, come forward, you gutless mongrels, and die with your leader!" he shouted. "Or return to your pretended king and tell him that the time of deception is ended."

The two dogs had no idea what had happened. They had seen the boy waving his hand. Then all of a sudden their companion had fallen to the ground with blood pouring out of him. That was no magic they wanted anything to do with. They spun around and fled, tails between their legs, squealing like two pigs toward the safety of their compound.

Matthew turned and ran for the Forest with the sword in his hand.

At the edge of the shadows of the trees, he found Raennel waiting for him.

"You were very brave, Raennel!" he said running toward her.

"I am sorry I did not stay to fight the dogs," she said.

"I did not want you to," said Matthew. "You did exactly what I told you. And now, look—we are back in the Forest!"

"Yes, and I am so happy! What do you want me to do now, Prince?"

"If you could just take me in the direction of the Tall Tree and help me find my way, then you shall go home to your family."

"Oh, that is easy! It is this way."

Dusk had deepened almost to darkness within the depths of the Forest when Matthew began to recognize where he was.

"I think I can find my way from here, Raennel," he said. "It is time for you to go home. Where do you live? I may need your help again, now that you have proved yourself with such courage."

"I live on the shores of Disappearing Creek. Everyone there knows my family. My father is Twelvepoint the Buck."

"Then go, Raennel, and tell him that you have come home to your father."

She did not need to be told again. With another word of gratitude, she bounded off and was gone.

Neither she nor Matthew had even noticed that the mist from the trees was not as thick as before. Some of the trees were no longer weeping!

TWENTY-ONE

Disaster at the Tall Tree

The moment Raennel was gone, Matthew ran the rest of the way to the Tall Tree.

He was surprised no one was there to meet him. The Council and two prairie dogs must be waiting for him inside. But how was he to get up the tree and into the den?

He looked about, but the lowest branch was much to high for him to reach it. He heard no birds, no sparrows, no monkey sounds above him. It was *too* quiet, he thought. Something was wrong.

Matthew searched all about the neighborhood of the Tall Tree. Then he remembered the tree nearby where Ginger and Spunky had taken him the first day they had spoken to him. It had branches low enough for him to climb on.

It gave him an idea!

Quickly he ran to it. Soon he was climbing high into its branches. He kept telling the others to be brave. It was now time for him to be brave himself. So he kept climbing higher than he had before.

As he climbed, he felt the trunk of the tree beginning to sway from his weight. Still he kept moving up until the trunk was not much bigger than his arm. It was swaying noticeably by then. When he had nearly reached the top, slowly the whole trunk of the tree began to bend. It was very dangerous. What if the trunk snapped off and sent Matthew crashing to the ground. It would have become a death tree then! But Matthew was desperate. He *had* to get to the Tall Tree! So he climbed another few inches until it bent over so far that his legs were dangling in mid air!

By then he was brushing against the branches of the neighboring tree!

Summoning all his courage, he leapt into the air, grabbed for the branches of the next tree, and held on for dear life. The top of the first tree sprang back up straight, leaving Matthew safely clinging to the second.

He had done it! And this tree was taller. Taking in a deep breath, he began climbing again, up and up until the new tree also began to sway and bend. Before long he was at the very top and tipping over and again holding on only with his hands. Again he leapt into the air. As dangerous as it was, again he managed to get himself safely into the branches of still one more adjoining tree.

This went on several more times. He leaned over and jumped from tree to tree, gradually closer and closer to his goal, until with one great final leap, Matthew found himself on a branch of the Tall Tree itself. He scrambled up and up and up its trunk—the biggest tree trunk in the whole Forest. At last he reached the hole into the trunk and the tunnel inside that led down to Crynac's den.

The entrance to the tree, too, was deserted. There was no sign of monkey guards, sparrows, jays, or woodpeckers. Where had they gone?

But there was no time to lose. Matthew crept inside, felt about in the darkness with his hands and feet until he found the ladder. Slowly he began the long descent. Within seconds he was climbing down in pitch blackness.

By now Matthew was used to his heart pounding. He had killed a great Doberman. He had been jumping about in the tops of trees. But now, all alone inside the hollow tree, an even greater fear clutched his heart. It was the fear of the unknown, and the silence of blackness beneath him, the spookiness of wondering what evil creatures might be hiding in the dark.

He tried to tell himself that he was being silly, that he was just imagining things. He had been here before. There were nothing but friends here. This was the Tree where the King's Council met. There was nothing to be afraid of. But telling yourself all that doesn't necessarily make the spooky thoughts go away. The important thing, however, is to be brave.

Down...down...down Matthew descended in the darkness. Luckily the ladder was strong, though the sword hanging from his belt made the going a little difficult. Eventually he began to sense from the air around him that the shaft was widening and that he was nearing the bottom. He began probing with his foot every time he stepped down. At last he touched soft dirt. With hands stretched out in front of him, and inching his feet along, he gradually made his way until he was standing on the floor of Crynac's den.

The air was cold and smelled damp and unused. Where was everyone?

This didn't feel right, thought Matthew. He couldn't see a thing. Then he remembered the candles. Mrs. Skunk said there were matches on the ledge above the hearth. He walked slowly about in the darkness, hands outstretched, fumbling to find the wall and the hearth. He bumped into a few chairs and tables, but eventually reached what felt like a shelf. He ran his hands carefully along it, feeling and grasping, until he came to a small container. Tiny sticks were pointing out of it. He grabbed one. The next instant the den exploded in light.

What met Matthew's eyes in the quick burst of flame was more shocking than he had imagined. The match quickly burned down. He lit another, this time and glanced about for a candle. Seconds later, Matthew had two candles burning. Now he had time to examine the den more carefully.

The place was obviously deserted. The fire in the grate was cold. Tables and chairs were strewn across the floor, their legs broken and tops bashed in. Pieces of smashed cups and dishes and glasses were scattered over the floor. A few pictures and carvings from the walls were broken to bits. The whole place was in shambles. The smell of abandonment pervaded the place.

Slowly Matthew walked about the room, anger rising within him at this invasion of Crynac's stronghold. How had the enemy discovered it!

Then something caught his eye that turned his anger to despair. He ran forward and stooped down. Feathers were strewn about—white feathers! With them were several splotches of dried blood splattered across the dirt.

Matthew's heart sank. He knew whose feathers those were! Something terrible had happened here. Matthew's body shivered with evil foreboding.

Suddenly he heard a sound.

It was faint but unmistakable. He was not alone down here! Someone, or *something* was nearby. Whatever evil had visited this place, the danger might still be lurking close by.

Slowly Matthew's hand went to the hilt of his sword. He had spilled blood once already today. He would not hesitate to do so again.

From the dark passageway ahead of him, footsteps approached. In the dim flickering light of the candle, he saw movement. A coat of gray came into view.

"Spunky!" cried Matthew.

At the sight of his commander, Spunky ran forward. It would be hard to say which of the two was more relieved at the sight of the other.

"What happened!" exclaimed Matthew.

"I don't know," replied Spunky. "This is how it was when I got here. I had no light, but I sniffed and felt about and knew that it had been ransacked."

"What did you do?"

"I waited for you, like you told me. Oh, oh—what's that?" said Spunky, now noticing the feathers. He crept toward them, then bent his nose to the dirt. "I fear that is falcon blood," he said

"I thought so," said Matthew. "Argon's allies have visited Crynac's den."

"Whatever happened, I'm glad you made it out of that place in one piece."

"Not without a little excitement. A doe called Raennel came with me. She should be back with her family by now."

"Raennel! She's the one who usually brought me food and kept telling me to drink the elixir. She escaped?"

"You should have seen her, flying across the field to the Forest, three Dobermans after her!"

"Good for her! I used to know her. She was a sweet young deer."

"She will be again. So despite what this looks like, hope is not lost. The Great Lie has begun to unravel!"

"What are we going to do?" asked Spunky.

"The first order of business is to establish contact with Ginger and whoever else is left, and find out what happened to Crynac. I take it you haven't yet been able to warn them about the plot on the King?"

"I've seen no one since leaving you."

Matthew thought a moment.

"Obviously the Tall Tree has been abandoned. Where else might we find the others?"

"Possibly at Shibnah's cave."

"Can you lead us there—through the tunnel from here?"

"I've never been that way," replied Spunky. "I've always come down from the tree."

"We have to get there, and you will have to lead. I can't see in the dark. Your nose will have to lead the way."

TWENTY-TWO

Through the Dark Tunnel

The way through the tunnel from Crynac's den to Shibnah's cave was long and winding. They made steady progress for the tunnel was much taller and wider than Earthshover's. This tunnel was large enough for a bear! But it was so dark Matthew had to move slowly with his hands stretched out in front of him. And Spunky had to go slow enough to stay with him. Left to himself he could have run on ahead and reached the end in no time. His nose was easily able to follow the scent of the path. Why the enemy had not also discovered this way was a mystery. As Spunky scampered along, he had to remind himself to slow down and wait for Matthew, and give him directions about what turns lay ahead. He thought he smelled Ginger's footsteps along with bear feet and fox feet. But it was a little hard to tell whose feet he was following because he also smelled Mrs. Skunk mixed in with the others. Though he would not want to speak disrespectfully, she did smell worse than the feet of all the rest of the animals put together.

They continued for what seemed like hours. It was also the middle of the night, and Matthew was getting very tired. He had had a busy and exciting day!

Suddenly Spunky stopped and came running back.

"Did you hear that?" he said.

Matthew stopped. They stood still and listened.

"Yes, I think I do," said Matthew. "What is it?"

"I don't know. We may be reaching the end. I cannot tell if what I hear is coming from friend or foe."

"Run ahead, Spunky," said Matthew. "See what you can find out. But carefully. And very quietly!"

Spunky scampered off through the tunnel. Matthew continued on, hands outstretched, one step at a time. Spunky was gone what seemed like forever. Finally Matthew heard sounds again. Gradually the flickering of candles and lanterns bobbed faintly against the walls of the tunnel ahead in the distance.

The lights got larger and the sounds gradually louder, until he saw Spunky running toward him. He was followed by Ginger and Barnabas the Fox and Chebab the Monkey and Mrs. Skunk and Mr. Badger and Widetail the Beaver and Randon the Wolverine, with Silverwing the Sparrow and a dozen more birds swirling about their heads. Before Matthew knew it a whole crowd was clustered around him clamoring to be heard.

"Welcome...welcome...welcome!" they all shouted at once.

"The prince is back!"

"Welcome, Prince Matthew! Welcome!"

"Let's get on to Shibnah's den!" laughed Matthew. "Then you can fill me in on what has been happening."

TWENTY-THREE

Doubts at the Center

As they were cheering and welcoming Matthew among them again, and shaking his hand and slapping him on the back with their wings and paws, Argon and Dezreall sat in their private rooms talking about the day's events. Though it was three o'clock in the morning, Argon had been unable to sleep. A glass of brandy sat on the table beside him. With hand trembling, he reached for the glass.

"What are we going to do, Dezreall?" he said, his voice quivering. "They have taken one of our children."

"Only one. It is nothing."

"But I was particularly fond of the young doe. What was her name?"

"How should I know? She is nothing to us—a foolish young deer. It means nothing."

"You have always said that our strength lies in keeping our family from thinking of their *other* families. Now one of the children is gone. What if more follow her? Our dream of a New Eden in the Forest will be ruined."

"There will be no more!" snapped Dezreall. "I have already instructed Sheena to spread the word that she was unbalanced and believed a lie of the enemy. As for the treachery of the idiotic sheep—everyone knows he had the brain of a peahen. No one will think twice about what he did. By the gods, Argon, get hold of yourself. You are acting like a child. We are still in control. The Forest will soon be ours. Then you can have your silly little doe and all the children you want. They will call you Father and King and bow before you and hang on your every word. Be patient. The Forest and everything in it will be ours to command. We shall at last learn the location of their garden and their secret waters of eternal youth. It will *all* be ours, and we will rule."

"But what if they find out my secret?" persisted Argon.

"They will never find out. How can they?"

"I don't know. But the boy the dogs described seems to have extraordinary, even supernatural powers. A great invisible weapon, no less! I am certain it is Matthew. If only we had turned him—he could have been great in our cause. But now, what if he finds *her*? What if she or her sons talk? They could expose us."

"Shut up, Argon!" shouted Dezreall. "They will expose nothing. Everyone will believe what we tell them. I want you to stop talking like this!"

"But what should we do?" whined Argon.

An exasperated snort sounded from his wife's lips. She should have laced the brandy with a sleeping pill, thought Dezreall.

"I'll tell you what we are going to do," she said. "We must act without delay. First, we will send our crows after the remaining boy and girl. Whatever so-called power this boy possesses, we will make him think twice about using it. Then we will set up a twenty-four hour guard to make sure the dogs prevent any more escapes. Finally, we must step up our plans for the invasion. With Ian on the way to intercept their ridiculous king, we won't have to worry about him much longer. It is time to launch our move and seize control. Tomorrow you will send messengers to Kaldorah. You will tell them: *The war for the Forest is enjoined. If you intend to participate in the spoils, send your army immediately.*"

"Are you seriously considering allowing the Kaldorites to rule alongside us, my dear?" asked Argon, his courage returning under the influence of the brandy and his wife's supreme confidence.

"Of course not," replied Dezreall. "But for the first phase of our takeover, we need their help."

TWENTY-FOUR

In the Den of Shibnah the Silent

Back in Shibnah's cave, Matthew was surrounded by a welcoming throng of animals all talking at once. Though it seemed like a crowd, however, there were only half as many as had been at the meeting of the Council in Crynac's den. Gradually Matthew pieced together a picture of what had happened.

As Beathnah's diversion had withdrawn and split up through the Forest to keep from being followed, a force of crows, wolves, buzzards, and vultures had invaded behind them. They had discovered the entrance to the tunnel of the Tall Tree. The wolves had scattered all the nearby ground animals, killing those who had been unable to flee, while the buzzards and vultures had penetrated the depths of Crynac's den. Fortunately, Crynac had been alone at the time or they might have lost more of the Forest's leaders. Somehow, though none of them knew how he had done it, the great falcon had prevented their discovery of the tunnel Matthew and Spunky had just come through to Shibnah's cave. A fierce and bloody fight had followed. Crynac had not been seen or heard from since. Several of their birds watching nearby reported hearing the crows squawking jubilantly all the way back to Argon's compound, *The falcon is dead! The falcon is dead!* Whether the buzzards and vultures had dragged the carcass back up through the Tall Tree, or had destroyed it, or done something unspeakably worse to Crynac's remains…no one knew.

The attack shook the entire Forest. Word of it spread everywhere. During Matthew's absence, most of the animals had gone into hiding.

"But the doe Raennel's escape from the Center of Enlightenment," Matthew told them, "means that the deception is weakening."

"I don't see much evidence of it," said Randon. "The danger is everywhere. The wolves are still prowling the Forest. Crows and buzzards and vultures come and go in shifts. We're being watched every minute."

"We know the situation is precarious," said Barnabas the Fox. "But we must take what encouragement we can. Prince Matthew is back among us. He is in possession of the King's weapons. We mustn't lose hope."

"By the way," said Chebab, "we have been saving these for you."

He ran across the floor and returned a minute later carrying the shield and helmet from the armory that Matthew had left with them when he had gone to sneak into Argon's compound.

"The King's Shield of Innocence and the Helmet of Purity!" exclaimed Matthew. "I shall no doubt need *all* the King's weapons soon. Thank you very much!"

"We have saved one other weapon for you," added Barnabas the Fox. "Shibnah," he said, turning to their host, who loomed large and silent against the back wall of his cave, "why don't you bring the prince the bow and quiver?"

Shibnah nodded. He returned a moment later carrying a bow and leather quiver of arrows.

"This bow and its magic arrows," said Barnabas handing them to Matthew, "come from the country of Aingard, land of Elves far to the east beyond the Forest. They were given as a gift to King Arze of the Northern Wars many, many years ago. With them came the prophecy that they were never to be used unless the very collapse of Pellanor was eminent. Otherwise they would bring destruction upon him who tried to wield them for selfish purposes. After we left you, Crynac reminded us of the Prophecy of the Bow. The Council unanimously decided that such an occasion was at hand. Crynac and I returned to Sogol Pell Lealnor for them. That was just before his disappearance."

Matthew nodded reverently as he took them. "I will use them only as you say. And not until all other means have failed."

It grew quiet. Matthew glanced about at his dwindling force of faithful followers.

"So what is our situation at present?" he asked.

"As you can see, our numbers are shrinking," replied Ginger. "We are under siege. We only sneak out by ones and twos for provisions and to keep news flowing to the rest of the Forest. But as Randon says, the Forest is being watched. Wolves are about, though they have not yet discovered Shibnah's cave."

"I see," nodded Matthew. "It is clear that the enemy has invaded the heart of Pellanor. But we are not defeated yet."

He paused thoughtfully.

"We do, however, have another bit of distressing news," he went on. "Tell them what you heard, Spunky."

Spunky told them about the plot on the King.

Growls and muttered oaths of anger and vengeance spread through the cave. What sounded like a distant rumble of thunder came from across the room. All eyes turned to see a look of fury on Shibnah's face, his eyes flashing, his lips quivering, his teeth visible and gleaming.

"We have to warn the King," said Matthew. "Yet this is your Forest, not mine—it is you who will know best what is to be done."

A sudden flutter blew into Matthew's face, and he saw Silverwing the Sparrow alight on Spunky's back and turn to face him.

"I will go out, Sire," he said. "I will do my best to reorganize my squadron of birds. We will set flight for the distant reaches beyond the mountains. We will search high and low for any sign of the King's return."

A gentle *cooing* sound came from within the shadows. A rustling followed, then a plump white dove glided into view in front of Matthew.

"May I go with you, Silverwing," said the dove. "I have done nothing very brave in my life, but I would like to try."

"You shall both go," said Matthew. "What is your name, Dove?"

"I am Branchcarrier, Prince."

"You are well-named indeed! You shall be sent out like your ancestor from the ark. Your mission will be different than his, but no less important. As you go, rally all those of your kind who are friends to our cause. I saw great geese in the mountain regions of the Garden. Their flocks can cover huge distances and will be able to search the farthest regions. I suspect the King will return through the mountains and come first to the Garden. But if treachery awaits him before he reaches its safety, he must be warned of it."

Matthew reached out and gently laid his two hands on the backs of the two birds.

"Go, Silverwing Sparrow and Branchcarrier Dove—go in the might of your cause, and with the blessing of the Prince. Find our King!"

He lifted his hand. With a great flurry of wings and wind, and cheers from the assembly, the two birds flew out the mouth of the cave and disappeared in the night.

It grew quiet again. It was Spunky who next spoke.

"Until they are back, it's up to us!" he said. "I want to know if there is a prairie dog-sized sword in the King's palace. If one of those wolves dares show his face in here, he will have to answer to Spunky the Prairie Dog—Spunky the *King's* Prairie Dog!"

"Remember what I told you before, Spunky," said Matthew. "The war, not just the battle. Your time will come. Until then," he added, glancing about then sighing wearily, "we have done what we can do for now. I am very tired. Shibnah, if you could show me where I might lie down for a few hours sleep, I would be very appreciative."

TWENTY-FIVE

Deepening Treachery

The two days that followed in the secret command post of Prince Matthew of Pellanor and what remained of the King's Council seemed slow and uneventful. There was discussion whether to remove some of their number again to Crynac's den. But as its location was now known and surely being watched, it was decided best that they remain where they were. Rotating guards were placed halfway along the tunnel joining the two compounds to be sure no snooping enemy spies discovered it and infiltrated their new headquarters.

Under Matthew's leadership, they waited patiently and renewed their strength. The time of rest gave Matthew the chance to learn more about the history of Pellanor, and the Lineage of its Kings and the stories of its great men and women.

Outside the hidden den, throughout the Forest, word spread that the prince had returned, and had brought with him the captive doe Raennel.

On the third day after his return, Chebab the Monkey came to Matthew inside the cave.

"There is someone to see you, Sire," he said. "I only hope he was not seen or, if he was, that his purpose was not known. He would be difficult to miss from the air."

"Is he a friend to our cause?" asked Matthew.

"I am confident of it," answered Chebab. "I do not think he could have learned your whereabouts otherwise. He asked for you specifically."

Matthew nodded. Chebab left him and returned a minute later leading an enormous light gray deer with a great head of antlers.

"I am Twelvepoint the Buck," said the newcomer. "It was my daughter you rescued from the Deceiver's compound. I wanted to thank you personally."

"Yes, Raennel!" said Matthew. "You have a brave daughter, Mr. Twelvepoint."

"Our family is whole again because of you," said the buck. "Raennel's brother is beside himself to have his sister free from the deception. I am here to place myself and my family at your service in whatever way we may help. We are yours to command."

"Thank you very much, Mr. Twelvepoint," nodded Matthew. "At the minute we are awaiting developments. I think the most useful purpose you could serve would be for your family to spread word in the Forest of what has taken place with you, to encourage them to believe for their own families. Tell them also to be ready to defend Pellanor when the summons comes."

"That we can do, Prince Matthew," nodded the great buck. Matthew had to lean back quickly to avoid his antlers! "And we will."

At the Center of Enlightenment on the edge of the Forest, things were in great turmoil. Those of Argon and

Dezreall's adoptive children who were more equal than the rest had been put on high alert to watch for any suspicion of murmuring and rebellion in the ranks. As a result, the Rooms of Healing and Reeducation were swelling with many who had been placed on a temporary diet of individual elixirs and their favorite foods and candies.

Suddenly their son Ian returned on the back of a giant vulture. Immediately he went to find his father and mother. One look and they knew he had encountered trouble. He was battered and bruised and walking with a limp.

"Their King had been warned," he said. "He knew I was coming and was prepared for me. I barely escaped with my life."

"No one knew of our plan but we three," said Argon. "How could he possibly have found out?"

"They must have learned of it from one of the traitors," nodded Dezreall thoughtfully. "This bodes ill. We must invade the Forest without delay. And we *must* have the younger boy and girl. They will secure our bargaining power with the older boy."

"They are on their way," said Argon. "Crooked Tongue the Crow returned this morning with word that contact has been made. Slipbill is leading them. They should be here this afternoon."

"Good!" said Dezreall. "I will begin preparations for a feast for this evening."

"What recipe of elixir will you prepare?"

"The same as before. What works for one member of a family usually works for all. The hardest part is getting them separated from their parents. Once that is done, the elixir will do the rest."

Shibnah's den continued as the center of increased planning. Their numbers were growing. The flocks of jays had not accompanied Silverwing and Branchcarrier in their search for the King. They were now patrolling the borders of the Forest, trying to keep hidden from the crows and occasionally leading them on wild goose chases if Argon's spies came too close. Frequently now the jays reported heightened activity at Argon's compound.

Late in the morning, Bluetail, leader of the jays, circled high above. When the coast was clear he dove straight down through the trees with reckless speed. He swooped into the cave so fast he nearly collided with Spunky, who was practicing thrusts and parries with a stick he had made into a sword.

"Hey, Bluetail!" he said. "Watch where you're going!"

"Sorry, Spunky. I have an urgent report for the prince."

Spunky turned and hurried into the cave, with Bluetail right behind him.

"What is it, Bluetail?" said Matthew, where he and Shibnah and ten or twelve other animals were gathered.

"I have no idea who they might be," replied the jay, "but less than ten minutes ago two humans were seen being escorted into the Center of Enlightenment. There was great fanfare and celebration. It was a boy and a girl."

A chill ran through Matthew's frame.

"What did they look like?" he said. "How old were they?"

"I could not say, Sire," said Bluetail. "We birds have a difficult time judging human ages."

"Were they younger than me?"

"Yes, Sire, and the girl considerably smaller than the boy."

"Did the girl have light hair, and the boy a curly mop of brown hair?"

"I believe so, Sire. But I was a good distance above them."

Matthew jumped up angrily from where he sat. "That charlatan!" he cried. "He will pay for this!"

"What is it?" asked Ginger.

"It's my brother and sister," said Matthew, pacing about the cave. "I am certain of it. They've gone after my brother and sister!"

Matthew grabbed the King's tunic from its hook on the wall and pulled it over his head. "How they managed to get their clutches on them I don't know," he went on, sitting down and pulling on the Boots of Truthfulness and lacing them up.

He glanced about. All eyes were upon him.

"I must return to the Center of Enlightenment immediately," he said. "I hope I am not already too late."

"I consider this a dangerous course, Sire," said Chebab. "At least submit such a critical decision to the Council."

"I must try to get there before they drink the elixir." Matthew said. "—Where is the sword?" he said. He jumped up and sent his eyes roving about the room.

"Prince Matthew," now said Barnabas. "I fear Chebab is right. You have spoken wisely of caution and restraint. Now it is our duty to urge the same upon you. We have already lost one leader. We cannot afford to lose you."

The next voice to speak was the last anyone expected to hear.

"The evil blackguard!" thundered Shibnah. "If I once get my paws on his scrawny little neck, he will regret the day he snatched my cub and usurped my fatherhood with his lies!"

All eyes turned in shock toward the great bear.

"I vowed not to speak," Shibnah went on. "But it would be foolish of me to cling to a vow if my voice on the Council can help. So I am ready to take my part with the prince, if it costs me my life. The prince *shall* go! We have tolerated the deception in silence long enough. I say we face the enemy to his face, look him in the eye, and renounce him. This may not be the final war, but it is a battle that must be won for the sake of the prince's family. I will go with you, Prince Matthew."

Shibnah's passion at once swayed the argument.

"You shall go," repeated Chebab. "I agree. With Shibnah beside you, my reservations no longer exist. I will accompany you as well."

"And I," nodded Barnabas.

"And I," added Ginger. "The entire Council shall confront the usurper."

"Thank you all," said Matthew. "I have never doubted your courage. But I believe this is something Shibnah and I must do alone. At present it is our families who are in the crosshairs of the deception. The two of us will launch the first blow. We need you three of the Council to remain here, and spread the word that the battle begins!"

"Whatever they do, I *am* going with you!" said Spunky, brandishing his prairie dog sword. "And nothing any of you say will stop me!"

TWENTY-SIX

The Rescue Begins!

A fourteen year old boy, flanked on one side by a hulking brown bear standing nine feet tall, and on the other by a gray prairie dog measuring two or three feet on its hind legs, left the protective covering of the Forest. They emerged into the sunlight and strode boldly across the open grass toward the red farmhouse known as the Center of Enlightenment. Immediately a host of guard dogs and wolves around the place erupted into a fury of barking and growling and burst toward them at reckless speed.

The three intruders came on steadily. If seeing a pack of twenty Doberman Pincers, German Shepherds, wolves, and Rottweilers bearing down on them with fangs thirsting for blood, frightened them, they showed no sign of it.

The first two headstrong canines tore straight toward them in full attack. The first, a huge brown Doberman, was sent twenty feet in the air by a deadly whack from Shibnah's paw as if a power hitter had connected with a fastball over the center of the plate. He fell with a broken neck in the midst of the charging attack, his comrades scattering in a yelping frenzy. The second, a bold Rottweiler fared better, though the wicked sting on the tip of his nose from the sharpened point of Spunky's handmade sword, sent him howling back to clear his eyes before trying it again. A great German shepherd flew at them next. Avoiding the bear, and seeing nothing so fearsome except a boy with his empty hand across his chest grasping at his belt, he leapt for Matthew's head. His fate was the same as the Doberman's several days before. A lethal blow from the Sword of Justice plunged into his heart, and he fell dead at their feet.

The company of dogs continued in a howling rage. But most now kept their distance as the three walked toward the house. A few who ventured too close found themselves leaping to avoid wide powerful swings of Shibnah's arm. They were confused how the boy's empty hand could be so deadly. But they all knew the story of the Dobermans on duty when the deer-girl had escaped. They had just seen the peril with their own eyes and were wary.

Without hesitation the three walked straight into the house. The noise of celebration from the direction of the banquet hall met their ears. The feast prevented those inside hearing the ruckus outside. As the boy, the bear, and the prairie dog appeared at one end of the hall, suddenly the huge room went deathly silent.

In horror, Matthew saw Timothy and Susanna at the head of the table opposite Argon, bubbly goblets in their hands. Argon was standing and was about to deliver the toast to the new prince and princess.

The silence only lasted a second. Before anyone uttered a sound, the roar of a teen age bear split the air.

"Dad!" came a cry from across the banquet hall.

"Dubpah!" exclaimed Shibnah.

The two bears lumbered toward one another, crashing over tables and chairs and sending children and animals scurrying in every direction. The young bear fell into Shibnah's arms. The father wrapped his huge paws about his cub's brown coat and wept great bear tears of joy.

"I'm sorry, Dad," said Dubpah. "I was wrong to leave home. I am not worthy to be called your son."

"Once a son of Shibnah, always a son of Shibnah," said Shibnah. "Nothing can destroy fatherhood. Come, son, we will go home and see your mother."

A commanding woman's voice interrupted the reunion.

"Dubpah!" it said behind them. "You forget yourself! Go and apologize to your true father this instant, and leave this big ugly lout of a pagan!"

Shibnah stepped back from his son and turned to see who had spoken. But before he could utter a sound, his son stuck his big bear nose straight in Dezreall's face.

"How dare you call my dad a lout!" he yelled. "This is my *father* you're talking about. He is ten times the father Argon will ever hope to be! You two are nothing but liars!"

Everyone in the hall listened stunned to hear one of their number rebuke Dezreall to her face.

The silence lasted only an instant. The roar of fury that now left Shibnah's mouth as he advanced on Dezreall, paws trembling and moving toward her neck, struck fear into all who heard it. Dezreall turned and fled the room.

"You cowardly witch!" thundered Shibnah behind her. "Stand and face your accuser!"

But she was gone. Moments later she was locked in Argon's private chamber gulping down a second glass of brandy in a single swallow.

In the banquet hall, in a turmoil and shambles, Argon stood shaking from head to foot. Timothy and Susanna sat spellbound to see their brother acting with such command, wearing a leather tunic, a sword in one hand, a shield in the other, and with a bow slung over his shoulder. They had not yet drunk the elixir and were able to see him as he really was. Argon, however, saw only a meek little boy. His blindness filled him with false pride and a confidence of superiority. He had no idea who it was that faced him.

Argon ran around the table to Timothy, then Susanna. "Drink of the delicious drink I made for you, children," he said hurriedly. "Drink quickly. Look, your brother is mad. The drink will protect you from him."

Matthew's fury erupted at last.

"Timothy...Susanna!" he boomed. "Set down those goblets. This man is a deceiver. Whatever he has told you is untrue. Stand away."

With trembling hands, Timothy and Susanna set the cups on the table. They glanced back and forth at the two, scared and confused.

Argon grabbed one of the goblets and tried to force it to Susanna's mouth.

Matthew leapt onto the table and withdrew his sword in a single motion. "Argon, you liar and pretender!" he shouted. "By the power of He Who Rules the Forest, I command you to stand away or die!"

"*Die!*" mocked Argon, who still did not see the sword. "You foolish boy. If you so much as touch me, it is you who will—"

No more words left his lips.

Suddenly Matthew's sword crashed down on the table, missing Argon's head by mere inches. But he had not been aiming for his head but for the goblet on the table in front of Timothy. The blade split the silver tumbler in half. The white creamy contents spilled over the white tablecloth. Instantly it turned black and foul. Timothy and Susanna screamed and jumped back from the table, for they *had* seen the sword.

Steam bubbled up from the spilled liquid. Out of its midst rose a hideous black form, spitting and hissing and flailing. Susanna shrieked in terror. Spunky dashed for her and pulled her away. The snake-like creature rose up high over the table, lunging at Matthew with long razor-sharp fangs, spitting fire.

With one swift blow, Matthew's blade sliced off the serpent's head. Something thick and black and oily spewed from head and body as they twisted and coiled to the floor.

Matthew spun again toward Argon. With another mighty swing of his sword, he split the second goblet in half. As it fell from the pretender's hand, it took two fingers with it.

A wail of agony rose from Argon's mouth even as another serpent rose hissing from the steaming spill. Argon fell backward. In another instant the second serpent's head was severed from its body, writhing in the stench of its liquid blackness on the floor.

"Timothy, Susanna!" cried Matthew, "Come with me. We are leaving this den of deceit!"

The room was in a tumult of yelling, shouting, and pandemonium. "Any of the rest of you who are ready to rebuke the deception of this place and go home," shouted Matthew, "—follow me!"

He turned and ran from the room, Timothy and Susanna and Spunky on his heels, followed by Shibnah and Dubpah. Clutching his hand to stop the blood, Argon shouted for his Dobermans and wolves. But after a few attempts to stop them, two more wolves lay dead outside with great gashes of bear claws across their heads, and three Dobermans and a German Shepherd lay in their own blood from the blade of Justice.

Outside, Matthew paused and looked to the others

"Make haste, Shibnah, Spunky!" he cried. "Lead them to the cover of the trees. Timothy...Susanna—go with the bear and the prairie dog! They are our friends."

Matthew turned and faced the house, sword aloft against any who might be thinking of giving chase. Shibnah and Dubpah, followed by Spunky, Timothy, Susanna, and four more who had *seen* the sword and tunic and had dashed for the door at Matthew's invitation, all made for the cover of the Forest.

The moment they disappeared into the shadows of the trees, Matthew turned and sprinted after them.

TWENTY-SEVEN

Tidings From Afar

Matthew ran up behind the others and threw his arms around his brother and sister.

"What happened?" he asked. "How did you get tricked into going to that place?"

"You remember the crow," said Timothy, "the one who came and talked to you and I didn't believe you. He came again and this time I heard him. He said you had sent him to bring Susanna and me to where you were. Since you had gone with him before, I thought it was all right."

"No harm done!" said Matthew. "It was my own foolishness that caused you to be taken in."

As they made their way back to Shibnah's home, father and son talked feverishly and laughed with one another, trying to catch up all at once on the two years Dubpah had been gone.

Reaching the Forest, great rejoicing broke out. Quickly news spread through the valleys, along streambeds, up and down the four great rivers, through meadows and thickets and pastureland, into the treetops, and all the way up into the High Country. It was not long before everyone knew about the return of Dubpah Bear, Redtail Fox, Wizzy Badger, Dandon Wolverine, and one of Mrs. Skunk's sons, who was simply known throughout the Forest as Stinky. What Raennel the Doe had begun, had suddenly grown fivefold! Pellanor was alive with the news from Alder Thicket to Fir Canyon. It was already being hailed as the Beginning of the Return.

The exhilaration from the daring raid on the compound, however, and the rescuing of five of its captives besides Timothy and Susanna, proved to be short lived. Some of those who had come with them had disquieting tales to tell.

As the Council of Four gathered the next day in Shibnah's den to decide what was to be done next, the mood was subdued. The cave was crammed to its limit. Sensing that the tide of the deception was beginning to turn, creatures had come from all over the Forest, some walking all day and all night to get there. The cave was not large enough to hold them all. Nor could it be helped, as more arrived by the minute, that the crowd spread outside the mouth of the cave. They stationed Twelvepoint the Buck and those with the keenest hearing outside so that any approach by Argon's wolves would be detected long before reaching them. Jays patrolled the sky a half mile in every direction. But the spies seemed to have been withdrawn for a season. There was no sign of trouble.

Mrs. Skunk helped Shibnah's wife as hostess. The two mothers bustled throughout crowded cave with food and drinks, beside themselves with happiness to have their sons back. But the discussion in progress inside the cave was somber. In spite of his initial skepticism, Randon the Wolverine, his daughter among the five, was now one of Prince Matthew's staunchest and most vocal supporters.

"Tell the prince and the Council what you told me, Dandon," he said.

The young wolverine glanced around the room, bashful to see every eye upon her.

"Go ahead, dear," said her father. "There's nothing to be afraid of. They need to know what it is like inside that place."

"Well," began Randon's daughter, "they kept telling us how happy we were. They made us say it over and over. And I was happy at first, I suppose. But if you asked about going home for a visit, Dezreall got furious. If you mentioned home or your family too often, they made you go downstairs to the Rooms of Healing and Reeducation. Sometimes you had to sit with them all around saying incantations over you to purge out the evil things your parents taught you."

Growls and mumblings and a few exclamations that cannot be repeated spread around the room.

"Now those rooms are full," little Dandon Wolverine went on. "They've been overflowing ever since Raennel ran away. After that there were many who started saying they would like to go home, too. The kitchen was busy from morning till night preparing elixirs and candy for them. I worked in the kitchen. But sometimes when they weren't looking I didn't put the little black seeds into the drinks and the other things they put in the candy, because I knew what a terrible stomach ache they gave you."

"What were the little black seeds?" asked Matthew where he sat with Timothy and Susanna beside him.

"I don't know," replied Dandon. "All the drinks are different, except for the seeds. We were supposed to put them in every drink. But sometimes I didn't."

"Good girl!" said Matthew. "That was very brave of you."

As the five youngsters spoke, they continued to reveal much they had been afraid even to think while at the Center of Enlightenment.

"I overheard Sheena saying something about taking all the rebellious ones to Kaldorah," now said Wizzy Badger. "They were worried that more would escape. I heard them talking about how the magic wasn't working as well as before."

"I thought they had taken captives to Liwanu and Amotan," said Matthew. "Didn't someone tell me that?" he added, glancing about.

"We had heard that," replied Ginger. "We never knew for certain."

"That could be," said Wizzy. "But I think they were planning to take them to Kaldorah now, so they would be far away from the King's land."

"I think many are already there," now said Stinky. "They've been sneaking them out at night so the rest of us wouldn't know. But sometimes when I couldn't sleep, I watched from my window. Haven't you noticed how many went missing and were never seen again?"

"Neighril was my best friend," said Raennel. "She talked a lot about going home. She disappeared about two weeks ago."

"I'll wager that Dezreall knows where she is," said Dubpah.

More growls went round the room at mention of the name.

"After what happened yesterday, probably more will be taken away," said Ginger. "They won't want to risk more defections."

"I heard something worse than all that," said Redtail Fox. "I was outside and two of the guard dogs were talking. There was a Doberman and one of the German Shepherds — they were arguing about whether the Shepherds or the Dobermans would lead the invasion when they marched on the Forest."

Gasps and exclamations went through the cave.

"Go on, young fox," said Matthew. "This may be extremely important."

"I pretended not to listen," Redtail went on. "They were also talking about the Kaldorites coming to help."

"They'll never take me alive!" shouted Spunky. "Why don't we attack them first, Prince?"

Matthew sighed. "Right now, my brave friend," he said. "I fear our numbers would be no match for them. What we really need at this critical moment is the wisdom of Crynac."

Almost before the words were out of his mouth, a fluttering of wind disturbed the candles in the cave and sent them flickering wildly.

"Silverwing!" exclaimed Matthew as the sparrow flitted in and came to a perch on Shibnah's shoulder. "And Branchcarrier!" Matthew added, as the dove swooped in and glided to the floor.

At the cave's mouth, however, a more spectacular sight awaited Twelvepoint and those clustered around him. Their shouts and exclamations brought half those inside streaming out into the open air.

Above them, a loud whooshing sound turned their heads toward the treetops.

There they beheld the feathery underbelly and outstretched wings of a great 747 of a bird, the most magnificent of Forest fowl, swooping in a downward arc. The wind from his wings blew a brief hurricane through the gathering on the ground.

Crynac glided into their midst, some feathers torn and missing, a few splotches of blood on his neck and breast, clearly scarred from battle, but very much alive.

A frenzy of exclamations spread into the cave. Everyone was talking at once and full of rejoicing and questions.

Slowly they returned inside. Crynac took his place with the other four of the Council, and stood like a statue. Like a true sage, he would not seize the right to speak. Wisdom never demands to be heard. As he waited, however, he cast a few piercing glances toward the more talkative of the assembly. His meaning was clear enough.

At last the cave was silent.

"He Who Rules returns," said Crynac wearily, though with no less command in his voice. "The warnings of our faithful sparrow and dove reached me high in the mountains. We were in time to warn the King and thwart the attempt on his life. But he sends word that his coming will take time. He says that battles against the enemy may have to be fought without him. What news do you have for me?"

All eyes turned toward Matthew.

"Speak, Son of Robin," said Crynac. "Your hour is at hand."

"As far as we can tell, Argon and Dezreall are raising an army," said Matthew. "We believe they are preparing to invade the Forest."

"It is as I feared," said Crynac. "On my return, flying higher than they could see, I observed a numberless force marching out of Kaldorah. I also observed great activity at the Center of Enlightenment. There appeared to be a column of prisoners being taken in chains in the opposite direction toward Kaldorah."

"The devilish coward!" roared Shibnah. "He is removing the children beyond our reach!"

"Peace, Shibnah," said Crynac. Then, realizing what he had heard, he glanced at the great bear a second time in surprise.

"You speak?"

"My son has been restored to me," replied Shibnah.

"Wonderful!" exclaimed the falcon, now first noticing Dubpah beside his father. "Welcome home, young bear!"

Crynac paused and grew serious again. "Events have begun to move rapidly," he said thoughtfully. "The house of cards is toppling. I fear Argon and Dezreall will grow desperate. It is time to prepare for battle. We must send word throughout Pellanor that the hour has arrived to fight on behalf of He Who Rules to save the Forest."

Crynac glanced around at those gathered with him in the den of Shibnah. They were still not many, nor were they such as the enemy would perceive as great warriors. Their numbers were comprised of the weakest animals of the Forest to the unseeing eye. But every one would give his life for its families.

"Only one assignment remains," said Crynac after a moment. "Our numbers are too few to fight on two fronts. We must both hold the Forest *and* rescue the children. Someone must sneak through the enemy lines to locate them. It may be the most dangerous assignment of all. But our only hope of victory lies in the power of our families being reconciled. The captives must be free or we will never hold out against the army of the deception."

Even as the last words left his mouth, Matthew stood.

"I will go, Crynac," he said. "At last I know the purpose for which I was sent among you, and that for which I have been trained. My mission is to help set the captives free."

"Wisely spoken, Son of Robin," said Crynac. "It is as you say. I knew what was your destiny when first I laid eyes on you. But you had to grow into that knowledge yourself."

"What is your will, Wise One? Should I leave at once?"

"I believe there is not a moment to lose."

"Then I will go," said Matthew, rising from where he sat. Again he reached for his tunic on the wall. The five members of the Council brought him the other weapons from the King's armory and the bow of Aingard.

When he was fully outfitted, Crynac bade all but Matthew, with Timothy and Susanna at his side, to leave the cave so that the Council of Five might have a few final moments with him. Quietly, almost reverently, the cave emptied.

"As you are not intimately familiar with the Forest," began Crynac when they were alone, "we need to give you instructions. From where we are now between the Redwoods and Sycamore Grove, you will know your way to the southwest border of the Forest where the Center of Enlightenment is located."

Matthew nodded.

"Liwanu, Argon's kingdom, is bordered to the east and south by Kaldorah, if that is indeed where they are taking the captives. — Chebab," said Crynac to the only member of the Council with the dexterity of hand to do so, "get soft bark from Shibnah. We will construct a map of the southern precincts of Pellanor between our present location and Kaldorah."

Shibnah disappeared into another part of his den. He returned a minute later with bark and charcoal. Chebab laid them out on the table and immediately began to outline the boundaries of the Forest, its principle rivers and woodland areas.

"You will have to determine which route is best," began Crynac, "both for learning the whereabouts of the captives and to reach Kaldorah. You will have to cross the Calumia at either the Sycamore Bridge or the Ford of Cullum...here and here," he said, pointing with his wing to the map which quickly took shape under Chebab's fingers. "From there, you may move either south or east. If east, you will come to the Southern River. You may find a small skiff at the Eddies of Logie. If the beavers are about, they will guide you as far as they are able and get word back to us of your progress. The river will take you downstream until it dries up. You must then be led by your own intuition. I cannot tell you how to accomplish your mission. It may be for you to locate the captives and then return to us for reinforcements. Yet without knowing what any of us will face, or where the impending attack will come, we cannot predict a strategy."

"I understand," said Matthew.

Within minutes Chebab's map was completed. Matthew looked it over, asked several questions, studied it another few minutes, then rolled it up and placed it inside his tunic.

"Barnabas," said Crynac, "bring the leather pouch in the oak box in the wall."

The fox returned a minute later with a small worn leather pouch. He handed it to Matthew.

"Take this with you as well," said Crynac. "It contains a few gold coins minted in Amotan during a time in our history when Pellanor was in alliance with the king of that land. They are very old, and came into the possession of the Forest Council back in the days of King David of the Meeting. As we do not use money in the Forest, they are kept perpetually by the Council for those rare occasions when we must conduct commerce with the outside world. You may have need of them. But use these coins sparingly. What you do not use, we will restore to the box for the next such emergency. You may get strange looks if you use them. Their markings will not be recognized. But no one in any of the neighboring regions will refuse gold."

Matthew took the pouch and placed it inside his tunic.

"It is time," he said.

The Council and the two brothers and sister walked out of the cave to join the waiting throng.

"What word do you have for us, Prince Matthew?" said Crynac as Matthew prepared to depart.

"Take care of my brother and sister in my absence," replied Matthew. "Train them in the ways of the Forest as you have trained me. — Timothy, Susanna," he added, turning toward them. "You can trust the animals of this assembly. They are your friends. They speak for Truth. — And to all of you," he said, looking about the gathering, "spread the word to hoist the standards and raise the clans of Pellanor. Be vigilant and ready. The battle is nigh. The defeat of the deception draws near. The reconciliation of the family is at hand."

As he disappeared into the Forest, the Council and all those with them grew quiet.

"Godspeed to you, Son of Robin," whispered Crynac.

"Amen!" repeated thirty or more voices.

"May the Spirit of the King go with you," added the great falcon, "on your lonely journey into the regions of darkness."

As the conversation gradually resumed inside the cave a few minutes later, none of them noticed that Spunky was no longer among them.

TWENTY-EIGHT

Alone Through the Wilds

As he set out, carrying a huge rucksack packed with food hastily assembled by Mrs. Skunk and Shibnah's wife, Fumra, Matthew began making his way south. The sense grew upon him as he went that his ultimate destination must be the distant region of Kaldorah. From all he had heard, he was convinced that was where the captives were bound. He must get there without delay, learn what was going on, and return to Pellanor with all speed. He sensed that the danger of attack was probably more eminent even than Crynac anticipated.

He reached the Ford of Cullum about dusk the next day. He continued on, bearing east, until it was too dark to see. He stopped and made camp on the western edge of the Fir Wood. He ate and drank with good appetite, then lay down to sleep on a soft bed of moss and dried needles. The night was mild and he was unafraid. The Forest had become his friend. If there were animals about, he knew that they were there to protect him.

Matthew awoke with the dawn, and reached the Eddies of Logie by mid afternoon. Seeing the mighty southern river reminded him of his journey up its thundering course to the Garden of Ainran. How he would like to see Miss Fernduddle again! But he knew that his way now led south. He saw no beavers, though many lodges rose from the wide shallows of the expansive river. He found a small skiff tied at the shore as Crynac had said. He untied it, climbed aboard, and gently floated out into the leisurely current. By nightfall the river was dwindling, overspread by great fragrant Eucalyptus trees bordering its banks. Matthew went ashore, tied off his craft, and found a place to spend his second night.

When he awoke the next morning, he saw how much the terrain was changing as he approached the southeastern reaches of the Forest. The trees had thinned noticeably. The ground was rocky and sparse of grass. He could obviously not take the river much further.

He consulted Chebab's map. The King's flask put him in the enviable position of not having to locate water as he went. He decided to set out directly east. He would skirt the northernmost edge of the Wastes of Kaldorah, then bear south and hope to arrive in Pellam City unnoticed. His chief concern was being seen by travelers along the main trade routes north and west. It was a risk he had to take.

He set out and walked east all day. As the sun was descending in the west, he spied ahead a small grove of stunted thirsty pines hanging onto life by a thread at the edge of the Forest. They offered at least some protection from being seen. His last night in the Forest he would at least spend under the comfort of what could be called *trees*, though he felt sorry for them trying to cling to life so far from the life-giving waters of Ainran.

He awoke the next morning and prepared to set out. Whatever protection the Forest had offered, he would leave it behind him now. He removed the King's flask, took a long drink, then turned it on end and poured the life-giving waters for a few seconds at the base of each of the twelve scraggly trees that represented the last outpost of the King's domain.

"Drink of the Waters of Ainran, faithful pines!" he said. "Drink, grow strong, and flourish as an oasis of the Forest. May you give hope to all who pass, and shelter them with your shade. May life expand again around you to reclaim these wastes for the Forest."

Matthew drew in a deep breath, then turned and strode out across the dusty rocky hills. With the morning's sun already hot on his left cheek, he set a course due south through the dry, rocky, desolate wasteland toward the region of Kaldorah.

TWENTY-NINE

Invasion

In the three days since the prince had been gone, back in the Forest Timothy and Susanna were having the time of their lives. They were a little young to grasp the import of everything going on around them, or the danger their brother was in. To them it was more like finding themselves suddenly in the middle of a fairy tale. Susanna spent her days scampering around with the rabbit and beaver and squirrel children, some of whom were almost as big as she was, and visiting their homes, as long as they weren't far from the cave.

Ginger and Barnabas and Chebab spent a good part of each day with Timothy, teaching him how to hold a shield and carry a sword and defend himself. They told him how important it was that he learn quickly how to be a prince of the Forest. And while he was more able to understand than Susanna that a war for the Forest was coming and he had to be ready for it, he was still likely to want to run off and climb trees and explore the Forest. Still, the three found Timothy a fearless young man, bold, trusting, and brave.

Thus they made steady progress, and were hopeful of making a warrior of him yet. Several thought to themselves that his destiny would lead him to take on princely duties of his own one day in the not too distant future.

On the afternoon of the third day since Matthew's departure, suddenly came the news they had feared, but not from the quarter they had expected. A huge Canada goose flew into camp almost recklessly, diving through the trees with such abandon those who saw him did not think he would make it to the ground alive. He skidded across his belly sideways, careening into a thicket. A dozen rabbits scattered in all directions, then came slowly back to see if the goose was still alive or had broken his neck. While they were doing what they could for him, one of them ran to the cave. Soon Timothy, Ginger, and Barnabas were carrying him inside. Timothy was the first to notice the piece of an arrow embedded in the underside of his wing.

"That would account for his crash landing," said Barnabas. "He was coming in on one engine."

An hour later, with several of the animal women clustered around him, he began to come to himself. He looked around wondering where he was.

"Where am I? What happened…"

"You just rest, Mr. Goose," said Fumra Bear.

"…got to get to the Council…important news…"

But the Council, assembled in another room of Shibnah's den, already had a good idea what news the goose had risked his life to bring them. A brief surgery performed with the precision of Crynac's claw had removed the tip of the arrow in the goose's wing. Crynac knew it immediately as of Shelaharan design. Minutes after he awoke, the women brought their patient into the Council chamber on a stretcher.

"How are you feeling, Goose?" said Crynac.

"I have felt better, I can tell you that," he replied. "I am Highflyer, of the northern geese of Maple Hollow. We patrol the Forest from the eastern mountains of the Garden of Ainran all the way to Amotan."

"What news do you bring us, Highflyer?" asked Crynac.

"Nothing good I fear, Wise One."

"We are listening."

"Last night, in the dead of darkness, we observed two columns moving into Pellanor, one from Shelaharan bearing southwest through Maple Hollow, and another from Amotan. It appeared to have crossed the border between the Shrinking Pool and the Dead Woods. It is moving directly south. At first light, we broke into two squadrons and moved low to learn what we could. Without provocation they attacked. I was above the Shelaharanites. Most of our number were brought to the ground by their arrows. I was one of the few to survive. Immediately I set out to try to reach you."

"You have been courageous in the service of the King, Highflyer," said Crynac.

He turned toward the rest of the Council.

"It would appear that the invasion will not wait for the prince's return," he said.

By the following morning it was confirmed by Silverwing, Bluesquawker, Branchcarrier, and Bluetail and their flocks of sparrows, doves, and jays that two columns of Kaldorites had left Pellam City. One was marching west through Liwanu. The other had already left the northern Shelaharan road and entered Pellanor, apparently in the direction of Alder Thicket.

Crynac nodded somberly as he listen.

"They come upon us from the north, the east, and the south," he said. "It is as I feared. The Book of the Prophecies speaks of a great battle where powers from the north, east, and south will invade the King's land. The prophecy says that they will converge on the Plain of Oddigem. It sits at the very heart of the Forest. If I know Argon and Dezreall, they believe that by seizing Oddigem, they will be able to control all Pellanor. We must sound the alarm, and summon every Forest creature."

That afternoon, the Council split into three groups. Shibnah and Ginger set out north through the Redwoods to rally the animals from the western woods and Timberlands before circling back with their force to the plain. Chebab and Barnabas set out south, crossed the Ford of Cullum, and made for the Fir Wood, before circling north. Bringing all the animals from that region, they would then move north through the Rain Forest, Chebab's homeland, where he hoped to rally many of the larger jungle animals to their aid. All the groups they could muster would then move toward the fateful Plain of Oddigem.

Meanwhile, Crynac and a vast fleet of birds set out to circle the four corners of the Forest, keeping high and away from enemy arrows, sounding the alarm that it was time for winged creatures of every kind to join them.

THIRTY

A Spy in Kaldorah

Matthew entered Pellam City, the capital of Kaldorah, through its northern gate. He was dirty and tired and knew he was a stranger in a strange land.

It was a *"city, with lofty walls and towers and battlements, and above the city the palace of the king, built like a strong castle. But the fortifications had long been neglected, for the whole country was now under one king...No man pretended to love his neighbors...There was one sect of philosophers in it which taught that it would be better to forget all the past history of the city, were it not that its former imperfections taught its present inhabitants how superior they and their times were, and enabled them to glory over their ancestors."*

As Matthew entered the gates of the human city, many peculiar looks from its inhabitants came his way. He wondered if they were able to see his tunic and sword and shield and boots and helmet.

Matthew wandered about the city all day. By then his provisions were running low. He tried to listen for any clue about prisoners in the city, but found the Kaldorah accent difficult to understand. It was a very unpleasant place. No one smiled. They all looked straight ahead as if their thoughts were consumed with only themselves. Everyone looked both sad and angry at the same time, like they did not want to be there but would get angry at the suggestion of living anywhere else. It made Matthew very depressed.

Hoping to learn if children were being brought there from Liwanu, he decided to make his way out of the city on the western road toward Argon's country. There were many soldiers about, also moving west. He didn't exactly blend in, but still no one paid much attention to him.

Several hours after leaving the city, he saw a dusty column of travelers approaching. Though most of the traffic was moving away from Pellam City, this large caravan was bound *for* the city. He hurried ahead to a small group of soldiers and fell into step behind them.

As the dust cloud from the oncoming caravan drew closer, a few figures came into view. They were being led by several men. Behind them walked dozens and dozens of animals—donkeys, dogs, horses, monkeys, cats, coyotes, squirrels and guinea pigs and rabbits in cages, and most every kind of animal you could think of, and dozens of human children, too. Matthew tried not to look too closely as they walked by. He didn't want any of Argon's people, or any of the children, to recognize him. The children and animals shuffled listlessly along staring at the ground. Their lips were moving. They were mumbling something. Matthew strained to listen.

"...happy here...we are all happy...everyone is happy here."

The column of captives passed. Matthew knew instantly that they had come from the Center of Enlightenment.

When they were out of sight, gradually Matthew slowed, drifted back from the soldiers he had been following, then all at once darted off the road and hid behind a great boulder. When the soldiers were out of sight, he returned to the road and hurried back in the direction of Pellam City.

In five or ten minutes he caught sight of the dust of the captive train ahead. He kept pace with them for the rest of the afternoon. When the outline of the city rose ahead, he quickened his pace. The captives disappeared inside the city gates. Matthew ran on. Entering the city with its bustle of activity, however, he lost sight of them.

He approached a woman passing by carrying a basket of vegetables. "Did you see that column of animals that passed by a few minutes ago?" he asked.

She paused and looked at him with a blank expression.

"The prisoners, you mean?" she said.

"I suppose so. They looked like they were being taken somewhere."

"Of course."

"Where are they being taken?"

"To the Valley of Serif Folleh," she answered irritably.

"What is that?"

"It is the refuse pit of Kaldorah."

"Who are those captives?"

"They are the Children of Pellanor. They come from the Forest. We have conquered their land. They are our prisoners now. The waters from their rivers will soon flow into all of Kaldorah."

"But who are the *human* children?"

"I think they are prisoners from Shelaharan, or maybe Amotan. I don't know. But children who cause trouble have to be punished."

"Who is it that you say has conquered the Forest?" asked Matthew.

"The Axis," replied the woman. "The Axis of the Liberation, the kings of the south and east, and the queen of the north."

"They have *already* conquered Pellanor?"

"The invasion has begun. The news is all over the city. Where do you come from anyway?" she said, eyeing Matthew with a strange look. "I don't recognize your tongue. Aren't you young to be away from home? You look like you might be one of them who escaped."

Matthew realized it was time he took his leave of this woman. He turned and hurried away. The woman stared after him, then looked about for a policeman or soldier of the guard. The citizens of Kaldorah were under orders to report suspicious activity.

But Matthew was already out of sight. He ran through streets and alleys, searching in every direction. But he could not pick up the trail of the captives anywhere. He arrived at the open-air market of a town-square. He took out the leather pouch and removed one of the gold coins. He then walked toward a booth where a bearded man was selling fruits and vegetables. He filled his rucksack with what he thought would last him a day or two, then handed the man the gold coin. The man took it, squinted and turned it over, then eyed Matthew skeptically.

"What are you trying to pull, boy?" he said. "This ain't no money I ever seen."

"It's gold," replied Matthew. "It's from Amotan."

The man looked it over again. "Maybe it is and maybe it ain't," he said. "I want to know where a boy like you got it."

"Where I got it is none of your concern," said Matthew. "It's worth ten times what I've got in my bag. So I'll expect a fair amount in return."

"If I decide to take your coin, you'll get nothing in return, boy."

"Then give it back to me and you can keep your fruits and vegetables," said Matthew. He began to remove what he had taken from his bag.

"Don't be hasty, boy, don't be hasty. All right, then, I'll keep your gold, but you'll only get ten *skipmas* back."

"Tell you what," said Matthew. "You can keep your change if you tell me how to find the Valley of Serif Folleh."

The man's eyes narrowed. "What do you want to go to a pit like that for, boy?"

"That's my business."

"There's nothing there but the Prison of Sedah."

"As I said, that's my business. Do we have a deal?"

"All right, then—the pit is south of the city," he said, pointing vaguely behind him, "in the badlands to the east, beyond the southern gate. But be careful, boy. Once thrown in there, it's no coming out."

Already Matthew was hurrying away, mumbling to himself, "We shall see about that!" He did not see the man, like the lady before him, leaving his booth of wares in search of a city official to report what had taken place.

THIRTY-ONE

The Prison Door That Was Not Locked

As Matthew ran through a deserted street, he nearly stumbled. He glanced down and saw a small animal that had nearly tripped him. He swerved to miss it again, but the creature seemed determined to get in the way of his feet. Suddenly it darted ahead, scrambled up the side of a wall, then stopped and turned to face him.

"That was a foolish thing to do, Matthew!" said the animal.

Shocked to hear his name, Matthew stopped and looked more closely. At first he took it for a chipmunk. But as he looked more carefully, he saw that it was a tiny gray prairie dog.

"What did you say?" he asked.

"I said giving that man one of the ancient gold coins was a stupid thing to do!"

Matthew recognized that voice!

"Spunky!" he exclaimed.

"Who else did you think I was?"

"But what are you doing here!"

"I followed you. I thought you might need some help. And I was right. We're going to have the whole city looking for us. You were supposed to keep under cover. Now you've as good as given yourself away. They'll know who you are in no time."

"But why are you so tiny?"

"All of us are smaller outside the Forest," Spunky replied. "It is only in the King's country that we reach our full stature. But come with me, we haven't a moment to lose."

Spunky scampered down from the wall and continued along the street. Matthew hurried to keep up.

"A woman back there told me that they have invaded the Forest," said Matthew.

"I know that. That's why there's no time to lose."

"Do you know where the prison is where they're taking the children?" asked Matthew.

"No, that's why I'm trying not to lose the scent," replied Spunky, flying along the ground with his nose down.

"It's out the southern gate of the city," said Matthew.

"And after all your questions, that's exactly where they'll be looking to grab you if we don't get there first."

They ran on. With Matthew's eyes and sense of direction, and Spunky's nose, they arrived at the southern gate and hurried through without incident. Following the road south for ten or fifteen minutes, they saw a huge deep valley opening on their left. At its bottom sat a complex of buildings. They turned toward it and descended a steep narrow path into the valley. Ahead of them in the distance they saw the column of captive children approaching the Sedah prison.

"There they are!" cried Matthew. "Let's go, Spunky."

They ran recklessly down the precipitous descent. By the time they reached the valley floor, however, the prisoners had already been taken inside.

"What are we going to do now?" said Spunky.

Matthew thought a moment.

"I think I have an idea. You walk on in front of me. Walk straight up to the gate."

"What are you going to do?"

"You'll see. I wish you were your regular size. He may not believe me. Wait a minute—what do you see on me, Spunky?" Matthew asked. "Do you see everything?"

"You mean the weapons, your sword and shield and bow and all the rest?"

"Yes."

"Of course," said Spunky. "I wondered why they let you wander about the city without arresting you."

"Don't you remember—they can't see it. But what about the Bow of Aingard? It's not from the King's armory. Do you think they can see it?"

"I don't know. I can."

"We've got to know if the guards can see it," said Matthew. "Well, let's go. We'll find out soon enough."

As they set off toward the gate, Matthew took the bow off his shoulder and strung it with an arrow. As he came toward the guard, who didn't see Spunky at first, the guard held up his hand.

"What's your business, boy?" he said.

"I've got another prisoner here," replied Matthew.

"Where? I don't see anyone."

"Down there...the prairie dog," he said, pointing toward Spunky.

"That little thing!" laughed the guard. "I don't think we need to lock him up! Why you got your hands up in the air like that?"

"I'm guarding him, in case he makes a run for it."

"Guarding him—with what?"

Matthew had found out what he needed to know. The man didn't see the bow! He put the arrow back into the quiver and placed the bow around his shoulder.

"Never mind," said Matthew. "But I'm under orders to take this prisoner inside."

"I'll see that he's put with the rest."

"I've got to take him in myself. I know he looks small, but this prairie dog is one of the watchmen of the Forest. He's an important animal. Don't let his size fool you—that's how he escaped. Now please, by the order of the King, let me through. I want you to escort me to where the prisoners are being held."

"Have it your way," said the guard. "One more varmint is nothing to me."

He opened the gate and led Matthew inside the compound. Silently Matthew and Spunky followed. He led them through several gates, then inside a huge gray building, down several flights of stairs, and finally turned the latch of a massive windowless steel door.

"Here they are," he said.

"I'll take him inside," said Matthew. "There is another prisoner I need to question. I'll let you know when I'm ready to come out."

The guard opened the door and they walked inside. The sight that met their eye was beyond belief. Hundreds upon hundreds of animals sat and lay and walked about in semi darkness as the door opened. There might have been a thousand or more! Those who had just arrived were but a tiny part of a vast throng. Who knew how long they had been in this horrible place!

They all glanced toward the open door. Matthew waited until the guard had closed it behind him.

"Is there a horse here by the name of Neighril," he said.

A few heads turned. Slowly a brown and white spotted pony came forward from out of the depths of the darkness.

"I understand you have a friend called Raennel," said Matthew.

"Yes, have you seen her!" said the pony. "They told us she was dead."

"Haven't you learned by now that you were being lied to back there? She is not dead. She was only asleep, as you all were. She is now alive again and well and happy and back home with her family."

"She is *home!*" said the pony, almost as if afraid to utter the word.

"She is, and she says you want to go home, too."

"Oh, I do. But it's too late. They've brought us here. They told us if we don't do what they say, they will make us slaves...or sell us as pets. And if we aren't cooperative, they say they'll make us stay in this dungeon *forever.*"

"That's not true. None of it's true. It is not too late at all. Would you still like to go home?"

"Oh, if only I could!"

"You can, and you will! Do you think you would be strong enough to carry me back to the Forest?"

"I am just a pony, but I think I can."

"Then we shall go home together."

As they were talking, a few more of the animals gradually came closer. At the word home, many turned away and began to mutter to themselves, *I am happy here. We are all happy. Everyone is happy here.*

Suddenly Spunky jumped up on the pony's back and shouted so loud the whole room could hear him.

"What are you all talking about!" he cried. "Nobody's happy here. You're all in prison—what are you thinking? You should hate this place! You weren't happy back at that Center of Enlightenment either. There was no enlightenment there. What made you listen to that liar and his pretend wife? It's time to wake up! You don't have to be here. You can go home anytime you want, home to your fathers and mothers and brothers and sisters—home to your families? Don't you know who this is? This is Prince Matthew! He has come to set you free, to take you back to the Forest. Wake up, you children of Pellanor. Wake up to the deception you have been part of. It's time to go home!"

It was a passionate speech. Even before he was through, the room was in a hubbub. Some asked questions and clustered around Spunky excitedly. Others turned away mumbling rapidly, *I am happy, I am happy, I am happy,* as if saying it over and over would protect them from the evil of Spunky's words.

"Who is ready to go home?" shouted Matthew. "We are here to lead you back to the Forest. But we will force no one to go with us. If you are truly happy here, and want to continue being part of Argon's and Dezreall's world of lies, you are free to stay. But the time to decide is now!"

He turned and knocked loudly on the door.

"We're ready to come out!" he shouted.

The door opened and the guard appeared.

"What do you mean by *we*?" he said.

"I mean we're coming out," said Matthew. "By the authority of the King of the Forest, I am removing these prisoners."

"What are you talking about! You can't—"

He was interrupted by Neighril coming up behind Matthew. She brushed against the guard and held him against the wall. "Would you like me to hold him here, Prince Matthew?" she asked. "I am strong enough for *that*."

"Thank you, but that won't be necessary, Neighril," replied Matthew. "He will not stop us. He knows that this prison is enforced by nothing more than fear. There is not even a lock on the door," he said.

Matthew turned back into the dungeon and again spoke loudly above the growing din. "Did you hear me?" he shouted. "None of you may know it, but you are not even locked in! They tell you there is no escape, that you will be punished and remain prisoners forever. But it is not true. You can leave this prison any time. Fear is the only weapon they have against you. But it is a false fear. What are you afraid of—your parents, the King, the good life of the Forest? They have made you fear the only goodness in your life. All you must do is admit that you were wrong for denying your place in your family. Then humbly rise up and return to your fathers and your rightful King. You may leave this prison at any time and be free. The guards here are under orders not to detain you. Now, who is coming with me!"

A great rush of animals poured through the door, with Matthew leading them in his train. As they surged through, with much bumping and excited braying and barking and shouting and squealing and squawking, the guard stood by and let the hoard pass.

"Lead them upstairs and into the light, Spunky!—All of you, follow the prairie dog. He is the King's watchman and will be your faithful guide."

The dungeon quickly emptied. With a great meowing and yelping and chirping and grunting and mooing and baaing and neighing and chattering and roaring, all sounds of great joy, more than a thousand pigs and horses and dogs and raccoons and rabbits and panthers and zebras and monkeys and tigers and birds and ostriches and sheep and goats and human children made for the door. Behind them, however, two dozen or more of their comrades sat huddled in the far corner, afraid to move, mumbling to themselves, *We are happy here. Argon is our father. Dezreall is our mother. Argon and Dezreall would never lie to us. We are all happy here.*

As the freed captives streamed past him through the door, Matthew gazed sadly upon those who remained. He knew he could not force them to leave the prison of deception. When they chose to return to their King, they would be free. Until then, he had to leave them to their fears.

When all who had left who were going to leave, Matthew hurried after them. Slowly the guard closed the door. It clanked shut, though remained unlocked. It would always be unlocked, though some would perhaps never come out. Only the King knew the final fate of those who chose not to come out.

Matthew bolted up the stairs behind the crowd of captives. As they reached the open air, he squirmed through the pandemonium to the front of the tumultuous mass.

"Follow me!" he shouted. "Your captivity is over. Freedom is at hand. Let us return to the Forest of Pellanor"

THIRTY-TWO

Retaking the Land

Matthew and Spunky led the freed Children of Pellanor up out of the valley. Instead of returning to the main road, Matthew set a northeasterly course into the desert highlands of Ianis. Though they had no *real* power to do so, Argon and Dezreall would do everything possible to try to prevent their return to the Forest.

Reaching the plateau out of the valley, with the city of Pellam in the distance, Matthew summoned the dogs to him.

"We need to find a protected dell or glen," he said, "where we can spend the night and remain out of sight from patrols that may be sent after us. I also need one of you to keep this vast throng organized. We must make sure we lose none of the children in the desert."

A dozen yelping barking dogs rushed forward at once.

"You, sheepdog," said Matthew, "—what is your name?"

"Fieldrusher," replied the dog.

"Good. Here is your assignment, Fieldrusher. From among your fellow dogs, choose eleven assistants. You twelve will keep order and keep us in a compact group as we move.—The rest of you, find us a site for tonight. But quietly! I know you are excited. But we are trying to keep from being found! Keep your eyes open, your noses to the ground, but your barking to yourselves."

The dogs rushed off in all directions.

Within minutes, the first of them began to return. Matthew went out to inspect their suggested locations, at length choosing one about twenty minutes away. Within the hour they were on their way toward it. It was so remote, in a small valley filled with boulders and overhanging ledges, that Matthew was confident they would not be seen. Their pursuers would surely look for them along the main roads rather than in the desert where there was no water for miles.

Once they were settled, Matthew took out the King's flask. He sent Fieldrusher's Twelve among them telling them all to come to him one at a time to drink of the waters of Ainran. At the mention of the name, a hush descended. As they came forward reverently, each bowed the knee before Matthew, then drank of the waters of healing and wholeness. Those who had but partially seen Matthew's tunic and sword and other weapons, now saw them completely. Now that they were out of the prison, they yearned for their families with a sudden intense longing they had not felt in a long while. Most had suddenly experienced fierce stomach aches after leaving the prison. They would all have to take up the sword, each in his or her own time and own way. But until then, the waters from the King's Flask soothed the pain and brought relief.

It took a long time for all to drink their fill. Then Matthew summoned various groups of the animals to enlist their aid. First he summoned the great birds—owls, eagles, ospreys, and condors—and sent out six of their number ahead to survey the situation in the Forest. Next he summoned six of the fastest ground animals—deer, cheetas, and tigers—with the same instructions.

"But," he reminded them, "you must stay out of sight. Whatever you learn, return to me with your news. Do not engage the enemy in battle. I am sending you out as spies into your own land. We must keep our force strong and united until our hour is come. The enemy must learn nothing of our return."

With guards stationed around the dell, the camp slept peacefully through the night.

They broke ground at daybreak the next morning. After strengthening themselves again from the Waters of Ainran, they bore for the Wastes of Kaldorah. The only difficulty lay in crossing the north-south road between Shelaharan and Pellam City. They waited until it was deserted, then crossed quickly and were out of sight again in minutes, moving northwest. Matthew was determined to press for the boundary of the Forest. As dusk descended, he sent the animals of keenest sight to lead them.

An hour after nightfall the report came back.

"We are approaching a grove of tall trees, Prince Matthew," said the raccoon delivering the message.

"What kind of trees?" he asked. "I know of no such grove in the Wastes of Kaldorah or anywhere nearby. Perhaps we have diverged from my intended course."

"They are pine, Sire. There are not many, but they are tall and lush."

The raccoon led Matthew forward to the head of the column. To his astonishment Matthew saw that they had arrived at the Grove of the Lonely Pines. The twelve trees had shot upward many feet in the short time since he had been here, and were now green and lush. A small spring bubbled up as an oasis at the center of them.

"We will camp beneath these brave pines!" said Matthew. "This is good news. The Forest thrives!"

The following morning, with great optimism and joy, the returning captives of the Forest families prepared to enter the Land of Pellanor.

Matthew summoned the human children who had come with them, some of whom were older than he was.

"The time has now come for you to return to your lands and your homes and your families," he said. "For some of you the way may be long. But if you are returning to your mothers and fathers, your way will be protected. The oldest of you shall lead the younger. Your calling is different than that of the Forest animals. Your lands have long existed in darkness. To you is given the challenge to rebuild truth in your lands by reestablishing the founding principles of your families. Be strong and of good courage. Tell what the true King has done for you. Return to your fathers so that the deception of the Great Lie will be broken among your people."

With much gratitude for helping open their eyes and for bringing them out of the prison, the children set off toward their homelands in Liwanu, Amotan, Shelahara, and Kaldorah.

As the Forest animals who remained set out, the young pony Neighril came shyly up to him.

"I have not forgotten what you asked me before, prince," she said. "It would be an honor if you would allow me to carry you on my back as you reenter the Forest."

"It would be *my* honor," smiled Matthew.

Being careful of his sword, Matthew climbed onto Neighril's back. With the other animals shouting and cheering—with animal cheers, of course!—Neighril and Matthew led them back into their homeland.

The terrain steadily changed as they moved north and west. Green replaced brown. Grass and shrubbery and trees grew up around them. By this time they were famished from crossing the desert, but there was now plenty to eat. Most of the animals could have made more rapid progress alone. Every one could have found his way home from here. But Matthew insisted they remain together. Their return was bound up in the future of the Forest. They must discover what was required of them.

By mid afternoon they reached the shores of the Southern River. The entire company broke ranks and poured into its waters, splashing and swimming and drinking with joyous abandon. One or two beaver children begged leave to depart for their families right then. But Matthew asked them to wait for news from the twelve who had been sent to spy out the land.

They did not have much longer to wait. Even as they were still enjoying the river, a great condor glided down toward them. Throughout the rest of the afternoon, more of the twelve returned. By dusk they were gathered again with Matthew.

All twelve carried the same report—that forces from Kaldorah, Shelaharan, Amotan, and Liwanu were closing in upon their brothers and sisters from all sides, and converging upon the Plain of Oddigem.

"The enemy's forces are too vast to count," said young Bupamah the Tiger. "They are far superior to those of the Forest."

"Enough of this gloom and doom!" said young Caleb Elk. "It doesn't matter how large is their force. We have the strength of the King with us."

"Yes," added Joshua Eagle. "Haven't you noticed how we have all grown since we drank the prince's waters and crossed back into Pellanor. My wingspan is twice what it was in that stupid Farmhouse of Enlightenment! Enlightenment my claw! The enemy's host may look gigantic, but I say that we will look like giants to them!

They cannot defeat the King and his prince. What is your wish, Prince Matthew? Speak, and we will obey."

"We must make haste to join our comrades," said Matthew. "We will rest for a few hours and get what sleep we can. Then we will set out at midnight. We will make for the Fir Wood, then bear north."

THIRTY-THREE

King and Pretender

As Highflyer Goose had reported, and the twelve spies had confirmed, four invasionary forces had entered the Forest three days before. They had marched through it unopposed, and had converged on the Plain of Oggidem in the very heart of Pellanor.

After word had gone out from the King's Council, nearly every animal in Pellanor had answered the summons. All were prepared to die defending their homeland. If this was to be the end of the Forest as they knew it, such it would be. They would make the Legacy of the Kings proud of them to the end.

Receiving the same reports from their scouts, Argon and Dezreall led the contingent of Liwanu troops north from the Center of Enlightenment along Songbird Lane and northeast around the wide bend of the Calumia. All the way they relished in their victory march, as they perceived it, through the Forest whose riches they had so long coveted. They were almost gleeful in the ease of their victory. This was *too* easy, they thought! Why had they waited so long? The Forest could have been theirs years ago!

But where were all the animals? Why was the Forest so eerily quiet?

They reached the appointed destination where they were to meet the four converging invasionary forces. At last they beheld why the Forest had seemed empty. All the animals were here! Apparently the fools were attempting an idiotic last stand against them.

Spread out on the Plain before them they saw their own allies from Kaldorah and Shelaharan, and Dezreall's countrymen from Amotan already engaged in battle with the ridiculously paltry force of a few thousand animals pinned between them.

The battle was as good as over already!

"It seems we are nearly too late, my dear," said Argon from atop his mount. "We would have needed but a fraction of these troops to defeat this motley assortment of creatures."

He looked about the battlefield. He was already thinking beyond their victory.

"Tell me, where should we build our new palace?" he asked.

"I will tell you when we find their garden," replied Dezreall, "and when I have drunk the waters of eternal youth."

Even as they gloated over the ease of their victory, on the battlefield heads began to turn eastward.

Coinciding with their arrival, or possibly having awaited it, a single rider came into view opposite them far on the distant side of the Plain. He sat astride a majestic white horse, huge beyond imagining. The rider was alone and in no haste. Coming down from the eastern mountains surrounding the Garden of Ainran, his steed stepped high with frightening calm. Every inch of his enormous frame contained the power of a harnessed hurricane awaiting its hour of revelation and destruction. Its great nostrils breathed in and out with potent energy. The eyes flashed as with blazing fire. The muscles of its mighty flanks rippled in the sunlight. The mighty animal was anxious to burst into gallop and tear the battlefield apart with its great hooves.

The approach of horse and rider, even from afar, drew the eye of every animal, every soldier, and every combatant spread out across the Plain of Oggedim. The rider was covered from head to foot in gleaming armor, his helmet of pure gold. In his hand he bore a scepter, also of gold, and the scepter was called Sogol.

Heads continued to turn. Where Shibnah was fighting beside his son Dubpah and his brother Beathnah, and where Randon Wolverine lay wounded trying to stop the flow of his own blood, and all around them Widetail Beaver and the family of Twelvepoint Buck and his cousin Whitetail and Brandy the St. Bernard and Mr. and Mrs. Skunk fighting side by side with their son Wizzy even if it meant dying together, and badgers and turtles and Jumper Hare and Bupamah Tiger and Gideon Racoon and Redtail Bear and all their weary and wounded companions slowly looked to the hills whence came their help.

The dust and frenzy and clanking of swords, the cries and shouts of battle and movement, all stilled. Dust settled. Shouts ceased. The stomping and snorting and breathing of horses and other beasts quieted. The squadrons of birds glided silently in a wide circle waiting to see what would come next.

An ominous silence settled over the Plain.

From his vantage point on a tree above the battle from which he had been directing his beleaguered forces, Crynac saw the approach as well. With two swift downward thrusts of his great wings, he rose into the air. He soared aloft toward the rider on the white steed. The rider lifted his arm. Crynac circled down. In spite of his huge size, he alighted on the rider's wrist with marvelous gracefulness, seemed to consult briefly with him, then soared aloft again. He swooped with eye-blurring speed in a great arc around the field of battle.

"It is the King!" he cried.

The word went out like a fanning fire of hope among the Forest host:

The King has come! The King has come!

The rider on his white horse rode calmly onto the battlefield, holding the scepter aloft toward his army. He rode slowly across the Plain and up the rise on the opposite side. All waited. The forces of Shelaharan, Kaldorah, and Amotan were so awestruck at the sight that they made no move to resume their attack. Their massive force spread apart to allow him to pass. No finger was lifted against him. A tremble of dread swept through not a few of them at the mere sight of the King's presence.

As he passed, now they perceived that his armor covered only the front of his body. His back was fully exposed. All knew that to strike a King when his back was turned represented the ultimate act of cowardice, and brought death to whoever attempted it.

As he rode slowly toward them, Argon and Dezreall watched with gleeful triumph in their eyes. Behind them, the army of Liwanu, however, did not share their mirth. Not a few trembled.

"The fool!" muttered Dezreall with contempt. "What does he hope to prove by this absurd display!"

"He has obviously come to surrender in person, my dear!" laughed Argon haughtily. "Perhaps he hopes that a noble gesture of obeisance will persuade us to spare his ridiculous following of animals. Have you ever heard of anything so idiotic—a kingdom of moronic beasts."

"The imbecile!" spat Dezreall. "He thinks to save his own life by such a surrender? We shall accept his surrender, all right. He will do homage to us. He will admit that we were right all along. We will strip him of his regal armor, bind him in chains, and then force him to watch as we make sacrifices of his following!"

She laughed derisively. "I always knew he was a coward, but did not take him for a fool!" she said, still laughing. "What does he think—that we will spare him if he begs for his life! I personally intend to cut off the head of that peregrine falcon of his, the so called Wise One. When it is over, we shall execute him last of all. As he dies, he will know that all he has done has been for nothing!"

As the rider drew near, their conversation ceased. But they could not keep smiles off their faces. They were enjoying their triumph very much!

The King rode up and reined in. He raised his visor. No one on the field of battle beheld his face save his two mortal enemies who had stolen the children of Pellanor, and had attempted their wiles on his own. He gazed straight into their eyes in silence, slowly turning from one to the other.

They smirked in delight as they saw the expression of love in his eyes. He was even weaker than they had imagined.

At last the King's penetrating stare came to rest for several long seconds on Argon. Husband and wife were utterly unprepared for the words that now came from the his mouth.

"It is time, Argon," he said with quiet dignity. "Are you ready to repent?"

Argon stared back dumbfounded. He could not hold the King's gaze. His eyes flitted nervously toward his wife.

"Dezreall," he said, laughing though his tone betrayed anxiety, "did you hear that? He wants to know if we are ready to repent."

A snort of contempt burst from Dezreall's mouth. She turned a look of unmasked hatred on the calm countenance of the King. Whatever vile imprecations may have been about to leave her lips, she thought better of them.

A pregnant silence followed. The moment of truth had come between the kingdom of light and the kingdom of darkness.

At last the woman of deception spoke the words of her own condemnation.

"But we've done nothing wrong."

Not surprised, in truth saddened, recognizing that a pronouncement of judgment upon herself had thus been spoken, the King hesitated no longer. He flipped down his visor in obvious preparation for war, wheeled his steed around, urged the mighty beast forward, still in no haste though knowing what the outcome must surely be, and returned down the hill the way he had come.

All around the vast plain his enemies sat watching his back as he rode. The King made his way again through their wary troops, crossed the Plain, and slowly began to climb the opposite slope he had descended minutes before.

Suddenly behind him, the wrathful cry of Dezreall split the air.

"Kill him!" she shrieked. *"Kill him!"*

The most expert bowman of all the Kaldorites, a great muscular Goliath of a man standing seven feet tall and weighing nearly three hundred pounds, raised the massive bow that stretched his own full height from tip to tip. Quickly he strung a huge four foot arrow. Within seconds of the command, the shaft was sent on its way. It flew across the Plain with pinpoint accuracy toward the unprotected back of the King.

Suddenly another sound rent the air.

A great *schwoosh*, which should have been silent but screamed over the scene of battle with a piercing wail, spun every head toward it. Another arrow had been launched from a knoll some four hundred yards away. With deadly aim, it intercepted the first in mid flight. A great *crack* sounded as the tip of the Kaldorite arrow burst apart and its shaft splintered into a hundred pieces.

THIRTY-FOUR

Defeat of the Army of Liberation

A ll eyes turned to see Matthew atop the knoll south of the Plain on the back of Neighril, the string from the Bow of the Aingard still quivering in his hand.

There was scarce time to take in what had happened. He quickly set a second arrow to string and drew it back. The next instant the Kaldorite Goliath lay dead on the valley floor.

The Kaldorites burst into panic. Suddenly from behind Matthew the shouting mass of hundreds of freed captive children came streaming toward them to be reunited with their families. As they joined the battle, the King reached the top of the hill opposite Argon and Dezreall and turned.

His great white horse reared mightily, pawing the air. Scepter in his left hand, with his right he pulled from his side the great Sword of the Ancients. Then across the Plain of battle he turned toward Matthew and slowly raised his visor.

Matthew's gaze met the eyes of the King. Could it really be!

His own…how possibly could he have…but where had he…and…and how did…!

A thousand questions assaulting the boy prince would have to wait. The battle was on! He had learned by now that there were times to *trust* what one saw, because Forest eyes were different than other eyes. All things were different here. They meant more than they could ever mean in the world he had come from.

Only one mighty word came from his lips.

"Dad!" Matthew exclaimed.

It was enough. For in that word was contained all the meaning of the universe.

The children surging to rejoin their families invigorated every creature on the Plain. From the most magnificent mammoth to the most miniscule mouse, all rose up as one. United again, the returning children of the Forest families grew to massive height and power, mighty at last to stand against the enemy that had stolen their affections.

At the sight of the army of courageous returning prodigals, the forces of Shelaharan, Kaldorah, and Amotan were filled with dread. Instantly they fell back under the onslaught. Their deception exposed for all to see, Argon and Dezreal turned and fled and made for their retreat south of the border. His keen eyes descrying their escape, Crynac again soared aloft and winged toward their so-called Center of Enlightenment. There remained captives there to be freed as well.

A great cry from his mouth instantly brought Joshua Eagle and Highflyer Goose and the Jay brothers Bluesquawker and Bluetail and a thousand more winged Forest warriors with him. Knowing the Battle of the Plain to be securely now in the hands of King and prince, they streamed south to free those who remained.

The deception was over. Darkness had passed. Light had come.

The battle did not last long. With Argon and Dezreall running for their lives, and fear struck into the hearts of the Shelaharanites and Kaldorites at the death of their Goliath, their armies were soon in full retreat. The Forest dogs all went chasing after them, barking and baying like dogs do when anyone runs away from them. But the rest of the Forest army, suddenly more vast than anyone had imagined, was happy to let the enemy go. There was no desire for vengeance in their hearts, only truth.

All around the rush continued by the former captive children to find fathers and mothers and brothers and sisters and cousins and aunts and uncles and grandparents. Never were there so many joyous reunions in one place. Tears and laughter and apologies and much forgiveness flowing all around. Soon came news from Crynac that the remaining captives were on their way north under massive winged escort.

From where he watched the scene, the King's heart swelled. Tears streamed down his face. For this restoration of the family, he had fought and prayed and sacrificed to the uttermost reaches of his own father's heart. This was the true meaning of the Forest. For the threefold unity of the family was the Foundational Truth of Creation.

After what seemed like hours, gradually the Forest host gathered and moved up the hill where Matthew and Timothy and Susanna stood watching with their father. By this time Neighril had gone to find her family, as well as her dear friend Raennel. Slowly the host on the Plain quieted and looked to their King.

"I congratulate you all," said the King. Though his voice was not loud, all heard him perfectly, even those far across the Plain. "I especially congratulate you young animals who showed the courage to return to your fathers and mothers. This was the victory won here today—not a victory against enemy soldiers, but a victory against those who would undermine the threefold cord of Pellanor. Yours was a victory for restoration, a victory against the Great Lie."

As he paused, a great caterwaul of animal voices broke out such as had never been heard in all the generations of Pellanor. They were cheering the King and his prince in their many diverse animal tongues. Yet with the humble simplicity known only in the animal kingdom but unknown in the world of men, they were celebrating and also congratulating themselves for their victory.

"And now to one and all," the King went on, "I extend an invitation into the mountains, into the Garden of Ainran. I invite you to drink from the Pool of Ainran and celebrate with me at Sogol Pell Lealnor. This has been a historic victory. Many of you still need to complete your healing by exorcising the seeds of the Great Lie you allowed inside you. This will be greatly aided and the process hastened with the waters of Ainran working wholeness within you. This will be an unprecedented gathering never before seen in the history of the Forest. You may enter through any of the four gates, the Gate of Fire, the Gate of Blood, the Gate of the Sword, or the Gate of the Book. Bring your wounded with you that they may be healed by the Waters of Ainran. You need only say to those guarding the gates, *I am on the King's business,* and you will be allowed to pass."

The King remounted his white house, beckoned the five members of his Council to join him, then turned and began the climb back in the direction of the Garden. Matthew summoned Neighrill, who approached with her brother and sister. Matthew climbed on Neighrill's back. Timothy and Susanna mounted the other two ponies. The three followed the King and his Council eastward toward the mountains.

THIRTY-FIVE

The Garden Again

Several weeks later, around the emerald pool spread out in front of Sogol Pell Lealnor, amid great cheering from their comrades and relatives, a ceremony was held for the presentation of special honors for what was now hailed as the Battle of Restoration. Medals were given and laurel wreaths laid upon the heads of Crynac the Peregrine Falcon, Lemmie the Sheep (whose leg was completely well, and who was by now a hero among all the sheep), Silverwing Sparrow, Branchcarrier Dove, and to those brave sons and daughters who were the first to stand against the deception and opened the floodgates for the rest to follow—Raennel the Doe, Dandon Wolverine, Dubpah Bear, Redtail Fox, and Wizzy Skunk. Two special presentations were made. The first was to Neighrill the Pony for carrying the prince on her back on his return to the Forest. Then a thin gold sword and leather belt, just his size, was given to Spunky the Prairie Dog. Henceforth it was called the Sword of Valor.

The celebration was bittersweet, however. Everyone knew that a time of farewell had come, and that they would soon be saying good bye to Matthew, Timothy, and Susanna. With full hearts and many tears, they watched Matthew remove his tunic and boots, unstrap the sword from his waist, and walk up the marble steps into the palace. There he returned them, along with the helmet, shield, flask, and Bow of Aingard, to the armory of Sogol Pell Lealnor for whatever future time, and perhaps future prince or princess, might require them—who could tell, maybe even his own brother and sister. When he emerged a few minutes later, to great applause and cheering, he appeared just as he had when he had first come into the Forest. Except, of course, for the expression in his eyes.

The afternoon advanced. Many tears were shed. The hugs and embraces and kisses and handshakes and pawshakes were emotional and numerous. The dwellers of the Forest who had come to love him so well knew that Matthew's time in Pellanor was at an end for now. He had fulfilled his duty. He had discovered who the King really was. And he had become a mighty warrior whose name and heroic deeds would never be forgotten.

When the presentations were over, Spunky, his new sword hanging proudly from his side, approached the King timidly but boldly as only Spunky could do.

"Begging your pardon, sir," he said, "and I hope you don't get the idea that I'm not grateful for your kind words and for this sword, but I can't help wondering why Matthew did not receive the biggest honor of anyone. He was the bravest of all of us."

The King smiled down at Spunky and laid a gentle hand on his head.

"Have no fear, Valorous One," he said. "He will be given the medal meant for him in due course."

THIRTY-SIX

The Giving of the Name

Matthew and the King were walking together alone in the high places of the Garden several days later. Most farewells had been said. The reconciled families of Pellanor had returned to their dens and trees and glens and meadows. The apes and tigers, pandas and monkeys were again at home in the rainforest. The elephants and giraffes and wildebeests and antelope had returned to their homes in the northern Serengeti. Sons and daughters had returned to their mothers and fathers. The Forest family was whole again. The weeping trees now lifted their leaves to the sun with rejoicing. New growth was bursting out everywhere.

"Why were you so long coming?" Matthew asked. "What if we hadn't known what to do, or had failed?"

"I came at the right time," answered the King. "I would not have allowed the Forest to fall to those who called themselves the Liberation."

"How could you have helped it if you were not here?"

"I was closer than you think, Matthew. I was watching all."

"You were *watching*? How…where?"

"The Great Lion and I were watching from the high mountains above Sogol Pell Lealnor."

"He was with you!"

"It was he who called me away during his hour of need. He accompanied me on my return."

"You were helping him!"

The King laughed. "Yes. A great danger had come to his land. I believe you know it as the last battle. As we are bound together by the Alliance of Ainran, it was not merely my duty, but my honor to come to his aid. That was some time ago. This most recent trip to the Lion's country was for a celebration of that final victory. He wanted to present me with a token of his esteem for my valor, as he called it, in his cause."

"So he was really here…watching our battle with you?"

"He was indeed. He said you were a worthy warrior in the cause for truth, and that I should be very proud."

"He said *that*!"

Matthew's father nodded. "And I *am* proud of you. You did well, Matthew, my son."

"Will the Great Lion ever come here—to Pellanor?"

"I fear not. There would certainly be great rejoicing at sight of his golden mane. But this is not his country. The fate and future, even the past of Pellanor, lies in the Lineage of *our* Kings. His story has been told. He would have little power here. All battles are different and require unique strategies. This is our story, just as that was his. Though it was similar in many ways, the battle for the soul of Pellanor was not the same as that faced by the inhabitants of his land."

"It is sad that the creatures of the Forest will never see him."

"Do you think so? I would say rather that it is just how he would have it. He was never one for long good byes or tearful regrets. Did he not say to make the best of every moment, and to summon whatever courage that moment demands."

"Where is he now?" Matthew asked.

"I could not say," replied Matthew's father. "When I rode down to join the battle, he bounded away up the slopes of the mountains. The last thing I heard before he disappeared was a faint roar, in which I think echoed the words, *Further up…and further in!*"

It was silent for several long moments.

"How was this battle different than his?" asked Matthew at length.

"This was an internal battle for truth," answered his father. "The war against charlatans who traffic in false freedoms and offer counterfeit pathways to liberation is a subtle one, Matthew my boy. It can only be won from within. That is why I stood back for a season and allowed events to run their course. You had to face the battle within yourself. I could not win it for you. In the same way, those on my Council had to learn to rely on their own wisdom, and on one another. They grew strong for the battle, as did you, by learning to discern truth from falsehood. I did not want you to trust *too much* in me to defeat the enemy for you. The battle against untruth is one *you* had to fight, and win."

"What *is* the Liberator, Dad?" asked Matthew.

"The Great Lie of Independence—the deceitful freedom that masquerades as enlightenment."

Father and son walked together in silence for some time.

"How did you become a King of the Forest, Dad?" asked Matthew at length.

"Ah, Matthew, my son," the King replied with a smile, "that is my story in the Annals. You will learn of it one day, for such is your destiny. But that day is not yet."

"How long have you been here? Are you *always* here? And if you...then how could you—"

Matthew shook his head in bewilderment. "Everything is so hard to understand!" he added.

Again Matthew's father smiled.

"You will understand," he said. "You have grown much in recent weeks. But you are still a boy-prince. You have much growing ahead of you. As you grow, you will learn about your heritage, here *and* there, about your future destiny, and your place in the Legacy."

"What is my destiny, Father?" asked Matthew.

"Haven't you yet guessed—you will be King one day."

"Me!" exclaimed Matthew.

"You will be my successor. Or *one* of my successors, I should say. We must not forget that I have *two* sons, as well as a daughter. Timothy and Susanna also have a destiny to fulfill in the Forest. All I can tell you is that you will all take your own place in the Legacy that will be written in the Book for future generations to read."

"When will those things take place?"

"Even I do not know that," replied Matthew's father. "Truth in the Forest is revealed by degrees, and only as we need to know what the next page of Life's Book reveals."

"Will you be King for the rest of your life?" asked Matthew.

"Probably not. The Kings of the Forest serve only until they fulfill the destiny to which they were called."

"How will you know when that is?"

"When the Council feels that my name has been revealed."

"Ginger told me something about that," said Matthew. "That's why I didn't know who you were—they never called you by name."

"No King of the Forest is called by his name until he passes on the Scepter of Rule to his successor," said

Matthew's father. "In days of old in the kingdoms of men, it was most often death that led to the coronation of new kings. Ambitious men murdered for the right to rule—killing to seize the thrones of others. The Legacy of the Kings of the Forest, however, is a legacy not of ambition but of service. When the Council and King unanimously believe that the purpose of a Kingship has been fulfilled, the Council bestows upon the King his new name. As such he is henceforth known in the Legacy of the Kings."

"How does the Council decide?"

"Any one of the five may summon the Council to meet when he believes the King's name has been revealed. The vote must be unanimous. If it is not, nothing comes of it. When a unanimous vote is taken, the Council summons the King. They tell him of their meeting, and propose to him the name. He, too, must agree. If Council and King are of one mind, the King begins looking for the right moment to step down. That time depends entirely on the readiness of his chosen successor. It is his duty to train his successor in readiness. Such training will usually already have been in progress for years. An additional confirmation of Kingship is having saved the life of the King—yet one more indication that the Kingship of the Forest functions on opposite principles from those in the kingdoms of man.

"When the King judges the time fulfilled, a ceremony takes place on the marble platform surrounded by the Waters of Ainran in which he passes on the Scepter of Rule. The new King then becomes known as *He Who Rules*. He serves until his own destiny in the Legacy of Kings is fulfilled. There have been two Kings who have served less than a year and then stepped down, three who died during their rule which required a different selection process, and others who have ruled for decades, even half a century."

"What if a King doesn't want to step down?" asked Matthew.

"In other words, what if a King becomes jealous of his power?"

Matthew nodded.

"There is no ambition in the Legacy of the Kings. No King serves the creatures of Pellanor who has not first plunged the Sword of Ainran into his own soul and put his ambitions to death on the marble altar where his name is first written, though not yet revealed. All princes and would-be Kings must also allow the Fire and the Blood to do their purifying work. *All* motives must be clean and ruthlessly selfless before readiness is confirmed. Service is the only law of rule in the Forest. Motives of self are unknown in the Legacy of the Kings. They are slain long before the scepter is passed on."

"Is the Kingship always passed down from father to son?"

"Often, but not always. Your great-grandfather, for instance, was not King, though he knows the ways of the Forest."

"He has been here?"

"Of course. He has many stories to tell!"

"Why was he not King?"

"He was not in the succession."

"But you were?"

"I was," nodded Matthew's father. "Nor are all sons fit to follow in their fathers' footsteps, or want to. Most can be *become* fit if they want to. Fitness for greatness is a matter of willingness, wisdom, and humility. Such qualities of character are available in abundant measure to all who desire them and earnestly seek them. But little can be done for those who do not want to follow the wisdom of their fathers."

A week later, Matthew, Timothy, and Susanna were completing their return trek through the Forest. They had taken the long way round so that they could visit Miss

Fernduddle. She had been so deep inside her den all this time that she was one of the few animals of the forest who had not known what was going on. She had to be told everything. That took most of a whole day—with many interruptions for treats and snacks for her three honored guests.

Then they continued on, seeing many friends as they went. Finally they passed the Tall Tree, and later that day approached the western boundary of the Forest. Walking tall with the regal step of princes and a princess, the two brothers and their sister at last left the cover of trees and walked toward their grandmother's and grandfather's house. All three felt many changes coming over them. They knew that they were returning to their old selves, though they also knew that they would never be the same again.

They made their way across the familiar field toward the house. Susanna and Timothy broke into a run. Matthew saw their great-grandfather standing beside the house watching as if nothing out of the ordinary had taken place.

"Hey, Matthew, my boy," said Opa Robinson, placing an arm around Matthew's shoulders, "did you have a good time in the wood?"

Matthew scanned his great-grandfather's face for any hint that he meant more by the words than he let on.

"Uh…yes, Opa," he said slowly. "I had…uh, quite an amazing adventure."

"Did you now?" rejoined his great-grandfather. "You shall have to tell me about it."

THIRTY-SEVEN

The Medal

Two nights later, lying awake in his room at his grandmother's and grandfather's house, Matthew was thinking about all that had happened in the Forest. The sound of Timothy's soft breathing came from across the room. Now that he was back in what some people would call the real world, he was having a hard time believing that the great battle for the Forest had taken place at all. On the other hand, when he remembered his conversation with his father in the High Country, he also wondered if it had perhaps been the most thoroughly *real* thing that had ever happened to him.

All at once he remembered his great-grandfather's medal from World War II. The adventure in the woods had begun so quickly after their arrival that he had completely forgotten it.

Matthew fumbled for his flashlight, then got out of bed and walked across the floor to where his suitcase still lay. He lifted off several shirts and trousers and probed in the dark until he saw the medal at the bottom. He lifted it out.

In the light of his flashlight it looked different than before. In place of the World War II emblem, the bright gold was emblazoned with the head of a lion!

Carefully Matthew set it beside his bed, then climbed under the covers again and turned off his flashlight, his mind full of many things.

When he awoke the next morning, the first thing he remembered was the medal. He sat up, turned on the lamp of the nightstand, and reached for it.

There was still a lion's head staring back at him. The features of the regal face almost seemed *alive!*

A tingle swept through Matthew's frame. Clutching it tightly, he ran from the room.

"Opa, Opa!" he called. He found his great-grandfather in his own private sitting room in the part of the house where he lived. Mr. Robinson looked up from his newspaper and cup of tea. His eyes fell on the medal in Matthew's hand. He looked into Matthew's eyes and held them for several long seconds.

Slowly a smile came to his lips, and he threw Matthew a brief wink.

"Is this your medal, Opa?" Matthew asked. "It's different than the one you gave me last summer."

"It is indeed, Matthew, my boy," said his great-grandfather. "And to answer your question—no, it is *your* medal now. I was given it to pass along to you for meritorious duty in the cause of truth."

"But I don't understand," began Matthew. "I think I am confused."

His great-grandfather smiled as Matthew sat down beside him.

"Everyone lives two lives, Matthew, my boy," he said, "—the life we are in right now, where everything is just as it appears, where we live and work and go to school. But we are also living another life at the same time. It is an *inner* life. That is where the great battles are fought. There the most important campaigns are won and lost, though few see them. It is there that the contest between right and wrong takes place, and where true warriors in the cause of truth are made."

"Why was I not given this medal with the others," asked Matthew, "—you know, during the celebration at Sogol Pell Lealnor?"

"Because Kings, their princes, and especially potential *future* Kings, must prove the mettle of their character privately, in their own hearts. Character is not deepened by being lauded. Indeed, the praise of one's peers is usually destructive to it. Humility is the mark of true and lasting worth. The Legacy of the Kings of the Forest is one of humility and service. Your medal was yours to receive alone, not amid cheers and adulation. Its purpose is to cause you to reflect on what manner of man you are becoming, and to quietly give thanks within yourself for the privilege of serving others."

"So *did* it all really happen?"

"Of course. What would make you think otherwise?"

"Because it suddenly seems so far away, like the memories are beginning to fade."

"Have no fear. They will never fade. Indeed, they will grow more real as time goes on."

"How could that be?"

"Because the inner is the *most* real of our two lives."

Matthew glanced out the window toward the trees across the field. They did not look so tall now.

"Will I ever go back?" he asked.

"Of course," answered his great-grandfather. "Your father, I believe, has told you of the Legacy of the Kings and your destiny in it. Not only will you return, you *must* return. You will be summoned when the time for your Kingship has arrived. Once a warrior for truth, always a warrior for truth. That war will endure until all is revealed at the end of time."

"When will that be?"

"No mortal knows, my boy. When this medal was presented, your grandfather and I were there with your father. We were told by the King of that land that our season had come to an end. But there remain other worlds, he said, yet to be won."

"All three of you were there!" exclaimed Matthew. "You fought together?"

"The battle for truth is one all fathers and sons are meant to wage side by side. Many of us who fought in that battle were sent back to our own worlds with the commission to be ever vigilant. Yes, your grandfather and I fought for truth together, just as you and your father have now done. We were urged never to forget that the battle for the King goes on."

"The King of which land?"

"The King of all lands, the King of the universe."

With much to ponder, a little while later Matthew walked outside into the crisp morning air.

A little way from the house, in the oak tree in the middle of the field, he saw a gray prairie dog perched on a branch halfway up staring at him. Matthew returned his gaze. Slowly one of the animal's paws came up over his eyes to his forehead, as if in salute. It lowered the paw, held Matthew's eyes another second, then slowly bowed.

The next instant the prairie dog scampered down the trunk of the tree to the ground, ran across the field, and disappeared into the depths of the Forest.

Other books by Michael Phillips are available from Amazon and at the website, FatherOfTheInklings.com in "The Bookstore." You may also like to visit Michael on Facebook , www.facebook.com/michaelphillipschristianauthor.